Falling Angels

of America

Mario Peeples riveting book, "Falling Angels of America," is a unique novel that explores a futuristic world where government graft and police malfeasance become so rampant that a secret shadow organization evolves to force the necessary changes. The story takes place in 2030 but it could just as easily mirror much of what is currently happening in today's world. —Author's Reading

Chapter 1

Mark Johnson was happy to be finishing his undergraduate degree from Hillhouse University in Birmingham, Alabama. He finished within four years in the Spring of 2030. The graduation was a rather impressive event. There were several speakers at the event, but the most prestigious speaker was a successful corporate attorney from New York City. Before becoming a big time corporate attorney, the attorney graduated from Hillhouse at the top of his class. Speaking at the graduation ceremony was his way of giving back. The speaker appealed to Mark's ambitions of pursuing a career in law.

After the last speaker said his words, the Dean called out the names of those students who would be Graduating in the spring of 2030. The Dean called about a hundred or more graduates before calling Mark to walk across the stage and receive his diploma. Mark received his diploma with a big smile and a firm handshake with the Dean. While Mark walked off the stage he looked into the audience and saw his family and childhood girlfriend, Sarah, watching the ceremony happily.

"I really am happy for him" said Sarah to Mark's mom.

"Yes, me too", his mom responded. "My little boy has grown into a man, and is ready to begin life in the real world."

"Yea, you know I plan to be there with him the whole way," said Sarah. "One day we plan to get married."

After the graduation ceremony, Mark took pictures of himself posing with his family members and his girlfriend, Sarah. It was a very special occasion. Everyone seemed to be hugging him or giving firm handshakes as they congratulated him and wished him good luck.

Mark was now one step closer to accomplishing his childhood dream of becoming a lawyer. His next step would be to finish Law School. In the previous months before graduation, Mark had applied to several law schools, however, only a few accepted him. He chose Virginia Central Law School over the other few small, but respectable, law schools. Virginia Central Law School was one of the nation's fastest growing law schools, and it also had a relatively large number of minority students.

He also had spoken with the United States Marines and completed an application to enter their officer program for candidates who wished to study and practice in the field of law. This option was something he considered, but he really didn't know if it was a good career path for him since a military career would likely constrict his freedom. However, the Marines failed to get back with him anyhow, which seemed to narrow his options to traditional law schools. Mark often wondered why the officer recruiting office for the Marines never responded, but he usually brushed it off and thought toward beginning the year at Virginia Central Law School.

When Mark made it home to Mobile, Alabama after the graduation, he was greeted by more friends from his old neighborhood. He yawned and stretched his arms a little as he talked with his friends, because he was somewhat tired from the three hour and thirty minute drive from Birmingham.

"Well, Mark, as soon as I am discharged from the Army in three months I plan to start college myself," said Martin Winslow. Martin was Mark's best friend since high school.

"Is that so" Mark replied. "Yea, you should have it rather easy Martin." "The military will probably pay your full tuition so you don't have to work," Mark continued.

"That gives me plenty of time to date and try to find that special girl," Martin stated excitedly ." " Hopefully, I will find one within my first two years of college." "Maybe she will be as honest and sincere as your girlfriend Sarah," Martin added.

"You will," Mark replied. Mark certainly agreed with Martin about his girlfriend being sincere and honest. In Mark's eyes, Sarah was one of the best women a young man could have at his age. Sarah had been with Mark since his second year of high school. She also cooked well and wasn't the least bit lazy with keeping a house clean.

Mark's other childhood friend, Harold, was quietly listening to the two talk about graduating from college and finishing a stint in the Army. He didn't have much to offer to that part of the conversation, but he was very proud of both of them. Harold was a high school dropout. He worked odd jobs and hustled on the side from time to time.

"Ain't you going to Law school Mark?" asked Harold.

"Of course, said Mark." "I begin classes at Virginia Central Law School in the Fall."

"That's good Mark."

"Yea, in three and a half years I plan to pass the bar and begin practicing law," Mark stated.

"Well, once you become a lawyer I may have to hire you to help me get out of legal trouble one day," Harold said quite seriously.

"Martin, how do you like the military life," asked Mark.

"It's okay, Martin replied."

"The reason I asked is because I applied to the U.S. Marine's officer candidate program." "Just to widen my options after graduation, Mark added."

"Oh yea! Did they accept you," asked Martin.

"Naw, I haven't heard from them yet," Mark replied. It was clear that Mark was still quite interested in the option to attend officer candidate school. If he was able to get a law degree through the military, his tuition would be free, he could earn money while attending school, and he would have a steady job after getting his degree.

"Well, I guess I will see you guys later," said Harold. "I have to paint a few rooms of a house tomorrow. This gig pays rather well," he added.

"See you later Harold," said Mark.

"I have to get going myself Mark," said Martin. "And again, I congratulate you on graduating from college, "Martin added.

Mark enjoyed talking with his closest friends on a regular basis. Harold and Martin had been with him through thick and thin, and he was also there for them when they needed him. He knew that Martin would always handle his business, but he frequently worried about Harold and his less than honorable side job in the streets. On the other hand, having a friend with street connections could very well come in handy from time to time for Mark when he finishes law school and begins his career as a lawyer.

There was the time in the eleventh grade when Harold defied school rules and came on campus to defend Mark from the members of a notorious gang. Harold hadn't been to school in almost three months when he came on campus and talked to the gang members while brandishing a thirty eight revolver. He made sure that no other students or faculty other than the gang members saw the street bought weapon when he threatened them with it.

The gang was after, Sarah, Mark's girlfriend. They wanted Mark to break up with Sarah so a member of the gang could claim her. The member obviously thought that Sarah had liked him, but wouldn't go out with him because of her relationship with Mark.

They backed away from the situation after Harold showed up. Harold was well respected in the streets, and the high school gang members had yet to do the dirt that Harold had long held under his belt. After the incident, the gang hardly even looked in Mark's direction or dared to talk to Sarah for fear of Harold's violent threat of retaliation.

Chapter 2

Sarah Jackson's apartment was a nice and comfortable little one bedroom apartment in Midtown Mobile. Sarah had the place decorated creatively with paintings on all the walls and plants in several places along the wall in the living room. She also had plants on the balcony. It was her attempt to make the place into a loving home for her and Mark. This is where Mark mostly stayed when he came home from college in Birmingham. It is also where Mark would be staying until he began law school in the Fall of 2030 and where he planned to stay on his trips home from Virginia Central Law School.

Sarah was starting to sweat a little as she cook Mark's favorite dish, red beans and rice, while Mark sat at the counter on a bar stool talking about all the wonderful times he had in undergraduate school. Mark partied a lot during his first year in college. He would club at least two days on the weekend and on college night at the hottest club in Birmingham. College night was usually on a Thursday or Monday. After his first year, Mark was all studies, but he still managed to attend most of the major campus events. When Sarah or his hometown buddies came up to Birmingham he would take them to a hot spot in the city.

On the other hand, Sarah was all business while she was in school back in Mobile. She attended Mobile Community College for two years, and received her associates in legal studies. She landed a good job at a local law firm as soon as she graduated. She was bringing in about thirty five thousand a year her first year and had the only income between her and Mark for the time being. However, she had plans on continuing her education and maybe even getting her law degree.

"You really done a good job on these red beans and rice sweetheart," Mark commented while wiping his mouth with a napkin.

"As usual," Sarah replied. "You know, orientation for school is in three months baby," Mark stated.

"I may get a temporary job for a few months, but a plan on doing a lot of reading for sure." "As a matter of fact, I'm going to the bookstore tomorrow and look for a good lawyer type book and then I will check with the employment agency to see if there are any good summer jobs available." "I prefer something in the legal field," Mark added as he rinsed his dish off.

"Well I can ask my boss tomorrow if they need any help at the firm," Sarah suggested. "Yea, that would be cool, Mark replied.

After all the dishes were rinsed and put in the dish washer, Mark and Sarah headed for the bedroom. Mark had plenty to think about. He had both long and short term goals ahead. One thing's for sure, he would try to spend his time preparing for the next three years to be spent at law school in Virginia. He would have to adapt since he had never been to Virginia before.

The next day Sarah got dressed for work while Mark was also dressing and grooming for his day at the library and searching for summer employment. The two didn't speak much as they departed on their day's journeys except telling one another that they loved each other.

Mark entered the library dressed casually in a striped button up and blue kakis and went directly for the computer library catalogue. He knew exactly where the catalogue was, because Mark frequented this library on his visits home from Birmingham. The library was a few blocks from Sarah's apartment, but it was across town from the library near his mom's house that he visited as a child.

After Mark sat down, he typed in general law studies in the field designated for subject. The results displayed hundreds of book titles. Mark wasn't quite sure where to begin so he scrolled through the titles slowly and picked the book that caught his attention most. It was titled "Law for Beginners." It was the perfect book for Mark, because he was rather new to the study of law. His undergraduate major was in political science and he had only taken a few law classes as electives.

As Mark stood up from the computer, he noticed some rather unusual looking characters checking him out from across the room. There were two men dressed in business attire and attempting to look as if they were searching for books, but were actually studying Mark's every move.

Mark headed for the area of the library where the book he had chosen to check out and take home with him was located. It was far to the left of the computer library catalogue and took him out of the view of the suspicious characters for the time being. He quickly searched the relevant shelf for "Law for Beginners" while looking to the edge of the isle for any sign of the two men. For the time being the coast was clear.

Mark relaxed for a while and decided to read the summary of the book to make sure it was a good place to start with gaining legal knowledge. He then quickly reviewed a few more books related to the law and headed for the checkout desk which was located next to the entrance.

"Are you checking out today sir," said the librarian. She was the typical librarian dressed conservatively with glasses that rested on the edge of her nose.

"Yes I am," Mark replied while handing her the worn book. The book must have been checked out hundreds of times Mark thought. He glanced over his shoulder and the two strange but professionally dressed men were next to the exit. One guy was facing Mark, who was still at the checkout desk, and the other guy had his back to Mark and was facing the first guy as if they were holding a good conversation.

As soon as the checkout procedure was complete, Mark grabbed the book and went out the exit to his car.

The two men who appeared to be following Mark continued to act like they were talking to each other but not without giving Mark a hard stare and a fake nod of their head.

After making it to the car without any incident, Mark decided to go immediately home. He was sure those two guys were following him, but he couldn't figure out why. He would surely tell Sarah about the occurrence when she got off work and might even tell Harold the next time he spoke with him. Maybe he should wait a while before he went out on a job search he thought or maybe he was overreacting. He knew he hadn't broken any laws so the cops wouldn't have any reason to be following him. Most law schools require students to have clear or explainable criminal records, which was one reason he made sure to stay out of trouble.

~

Mark and Harold walked toward the entrance of the city employment office at a modest pace. Mark looked straight ahead as Harold surveyed the surroundings as they walked. Harold was wearing some dark shades known as locs to most of the younger generation. They were so dark that people couldn't tell which direction the person wearing them was looking. So far, nothing seemed to be out of the ordinary.

Harold had come along for two reasons. One reason was to look for a job and the other reason was for security since Mark had concluded someone was following him on the previous day at the library.

"You say they were dressed in business suits," Harold whispered to Mark.

"Yea," Mark replied. "They may be hired by that long sharp that I borrowed money from to bet on the Super Bowl last winter. You know I lost and wasn't able to repay the sharp."

Harold stopped for a second and looked at Mark. "Well I'm not worried about them, but if it happens to be detectives or some other law enforcement, you're on your own. I don't mess with cops," Harold affirmed while slightly raising his shades above his eyes.

As soon as they walked through the door, Mark noticed a recruiting booth for the United States Marine Corp set up in the left corner of the employment office. It wasn't for officer recruiting, but Mark thought he definitely wanted to speak with the recruiting officers concerning the application he put in for their officer law program. The officer recruiters in Birmingham had failed to follow up with him about his application, and all efforts to contact them were unsuccessful.

As he approached the booth with Harold keeping a slight distance, Mark couldn't help but to realize that the two recruiters were only slightly older than him and probably had yet to obtain an undergraduate degree in any field. One recruiter was a noncommissioned officer and the other one was of a much lower rank.

"Are you interested in signing up for the Marines today sir," asked the lower ranked Marine enthusiastically.

"No, actually I applied for officer candidate school several months ago in Birmingham, but I wasn't notified of a decision yet," Mark replied. He knew the situation was a little more complex than that. The officer recruiting office hadn't even answered the phone since he applied. He had started to assume that the recruiting officers could tell that he wasn't sure about his future plans after college.

"That's unusual. An officer should have contacted you within a month after receiving your application," said the noncommissioned officer. "I'll tell you what. Give me your full name, and I will contact the office in Birmingham and see what's going on," he insured Mark in an attempt to end the conversation. The recruiter sensed that there was some sort of problem with Mark's application. Mark quickly jotted his name on a legal pad and gave it to the recruiter.

Harold had already sat at a computer to update his file and perform a job search. He kept a frequent watch on Mark and surveyed the scene at employment office to make sure no one was stalking them while he and Mark viewed the jobs database for the Mobile County area. Most of Harold's experience was in hustling and other street related occupations, but he also had learned the construction trade considerably in the last few years, so as soon as he saw a position in that field, he immediately jotted down the contact information. He continued this procedure for almost thirty minutes, and accumulated a list of about five contacts while applying for one position online. The job was for a tool room attendant at a large construction site located about twenty minutes from Mobile.

Feeling quite confident about his self, Harold politely slid his chair under the table and moved four chairs down to an empty chair next to Mark, who was reading the job qualifications required for an interesting job at the local legal aid foundation. The position was perfect for Mark. It was designated for applicants seeking summer employment and those who aspired to obtain a law degree. It was only one of two positions in the database that interested Mark and the only job that would end just before he started law school.

After deciding that he met all of the qualifications for the job, Mark emailed a copy of his cover letter and resume to the appropriate email address. The other interesting job was for a runner at a midlevel law firm in the center of downtown. It required applicants to mail a professional cover letter and resume to the firm's downtown address. Mark didn't have his hopes up high for that one though, because he knew there weren't many minorities in the larger law firms in Mobile. However, he still planned to give it a try. He knew he probably had a better chance getting hired by the legal aid foundation or at Sarah's firm. There were two partners at the law firm where Sarah worked, and both of them were African American. No matter what color his bosses would be, Mark planned to take the first job offer if given an opportunity.

Once Mark was done with his job search, he and Harold quietly walked out of the employment office. As they walked out, a lady sitting behind the desk waved and politely said "Have a nice day." Once outside, Harold put his shades back on and began surveying the parking lot for any suspicious characters. They had almost made it to the car when Mark bumped Harold and nodded to the right in an effort to get him to look in that direction. There were two men sitting in a Chevrolet sedan with slightly tinted windows. One guy was black and the other guy was white. Both were in their early forties. The tag had regular plates, but there were several antennas sticking up from the trunk.

"That's the same guys from the library," Mark mumbled to Harold.

"Yo, those guys look like cops Mark," Harold replied in a low tone. "Not just any cops either. The kind that investigates drug dealers and murder suspects or any other major felony crime," he added.

"Maybe, but I haven't done any illegal activity besides drinking in public and a little gambling every now and then," Mark replied.

"I'm not messing with those guys, but I don't think you have to worry about them trying to harm you besides putting some handcuffs on too tight," Harold joked with Mark while getting in the car.

Chapter 3

Mark was sitting on the couch of Sarah's apartment looking through the Virginia Central Law School catalogue when Sarah came through the door looking exhausted, but it was also obvious that she had something to reveal to Mark by her sneaky but lovely smile.

"How was your day at work today baby," Mark asked Sarah.

"It was pretty good Sarah replied. Busy as usual. I asked Mr. Cunningham if he could use any help around the office. I told him you were looking for something temporary until the school term started."

"Really, what did he say?" "He said sure, but he couldn't pay you more than twelve dollars an hour, and he could only use you part time."

"That would be great," Mark responded excitedly. "I still have a considerable savings account to complement my income so part time would be fine. Hold on. You don't think that would interfere with our relationship do you," Mark asked. "I mean, spending that much time around each other."

"Absolutely not," Sarah assured him with a loving smile.

The firm where Sarah worked was a black owned firm that went by the name of Jones and Cunningham. Alan Jones and Kevin Cunningham were both graduates of Southern University Law Center. They went to work at separate firms for a few years after graduating before they decided to form their own law firm. They figured they could better serve their purpose by branching out on their own and still make a decent paycheck after paying the bills.

Mark's job duties would be rather general, but it still would be close enough to the field of law for him to get his feet wet. Some of his duties would range from running the copier to interviewing potential clients concerning their cases. He also hoped that the legal assistants there would introduce him to, writing legal briefs, something that would give him a head start on the first year law students.

"Sarah, what will be my dress code for this temporary and part time position at the office," Mark asked. "I can't help but realize that you be dressed to perfection and looking good everyday you go to work."

"Well, most days you can dress casual, but sometimes a suit will be required. Especially if you're going to be in the courtroom," Sarah responded.

"That's fine. I have about three decent suits that I could dress in when necessary," Mark stated.

For a while Mark thought about mentioning the two odd guys that were following him when he went to the library and unemployment office, but he didn't want to worry her. Instead, he hugged for a while with his hands gripping the lower of her hips. He sweetly asked her what she wanted for dinner while swirling the car keys in his hand. She insisted on a large order of shrimp fried Chinese rice, and that is exactly what Mark would grab. He really liked satisfying Sarah as much as he could.

~

Mark had just finished his first week of work, when Martin called to ask Mark if he wanted to go to a bar for a few drinks. Mark's first week at the firm was spent getting him familiar with the duties he would be entrusted to do while he was employed there. While Mark had just begun, the stress of learning the responsibilities of a new job made Martin's offer for a chance to get out and enjoy themselves sound rather appealing.

Mark and Martin took a seat towards the end of the bar. Mark was dressed in a button up shirt and cream colored kakis, the same clothes he went to work in. Martin sported blue jeans with a grey designer t-shirt. The bartender was a tan skinned white male in his late forties. "What can I get you two gentlemen this evening," the bartender asked.

"Let us get two ice cold draft beers," Martin replied.

"I just need to see your IDs fellas," the bartender asked nicely. Both Martin and Mark were still in their early twenties and barely looked their age. Mark had a slight mustache and beard, but Martin was clean shaven as required by the army. The two handed the bartender their Driver's Licenses as they slid the frosted bottles of beer closer. Mark turned his bottle up as soon as the bartender handed his Driver's License back. He took about three gulps before placing down on the counter. Martin took a slight sip before starting to comment on Mark's success with finding a job.

"So your girl got you your first job since graduating huh," Martin gestured to Mark with a wide smile.

"Yea, it's just a part time gig, but it will give me a good chance to get familiar with the legal field," Mark replied. "It was either something related to my undergraduate degree in political science or something related to my future educational plans in law," he continued.

"So how much longer you got serving our country in the armed forces," Mark asked.

"I'm officially out in about two months on July 19th. That will be a full four years for me in a very strict environment with little privacy," Martin responded.

"Yea, I heard that you can get disciplined for cheating on your wife. Luckily, you were not married yet buddy," Mark added while laughing a little.

While Mark stayed with the same girl after graduating high school, Martin switched women like he changed clothes. It seemed as if he had a new girlfriend every other month of the year during his four year stint in the army. There was a different girl every time he visited Mark while he was in college, causing Sarah to become very concerned with her relationship with Mark whenever he and Martin hung out together.

While the two talked there were several TVs playing in the lounge. Three were above and behind the bar that Mark and Martin was sitting at. Two of the televisions behind the bar were showing some old college baseball game and the other was playing the CNN news station. The volumes on all three TVs were up enough that you could hear them if you zoomed in on a particular TV. As Martin continued to talk about some of the sexual adventures that he experienced when he was stationed in South Korea, Mark had caught a sudden interest in the TV playing the cable news channel.

The new anchorwoman was interviewing the current United States Attorney General, Ervin Mills. Attorney General Mills had been in his position since being easily nominated after President Harding took office in January. He was half Chinese American and half African American, and was one of three minorities on the President's Cabinet. President Charles Harding, himself, was Caucasian but had a mixture of European ancestors which included Irish, English, and Jewish roots.

Mark thought about how cool it was for the United States to have an Attorney General with African American heritage. Attorney General Mills was only the third African American Attorney General in the history of America. With hard work and determination, Mark thought it was even possible for him to achieve such status in the legal field.

After noticing that Mark wasn't paying attention to what he was talking about anymore, Martin joined Mark with watching the CNN news interview. Martin, being in the Army and all, was very familiar with the country's current administration, including Attorney General Mills. Mills was answering questions concerning the state of new technological advancements being used by the government. In particular, he hinted on a very useful technology being developed, but he wouldn't go into detail. He only suggested that it could change the way the country operated.

"Do you have any idea what world changing technology he could be talking about," Mark asked Martin.

"Not really. It's probably top secret now. You know, only reserved for top ranked government officials and people like that," Martin replied. "We have lots of confidential technology secrets in the military, but he may be talking about technology specific to law enforcement agencies such as the Justice Department and the FBI."

By now, the two were on their third cold beer a piece, and was pretty much at their limit. Neither Mark nor Martin was even slightly impaired though. They both could probably handle twice as much before they reached that point, but for driving purposes, they decided to call it quits early. They never knew when some hotshot cop might decide to pull them over and give them a breath analyzer. A DUI would be a catastrophe for Mark and Martin, with Mark trying to start law school and Martin only two months away from getting an honorable discharge.

Mark tipped the bartender with a five dollar bill as the two got up and exited the bar in somewhat of a cheerful mood. The sun was just beginning to set as each of the guys went to their cars. Mark told Martin that he would catch up with him later before starting his car and turning on the headlights.

A few minutes after Mark pulled off, he noticed a set of headlights behind him following unusually close. He knew it wasn't Martin, because Martin had went in the other direction to get on the interstate. He had about a twenty minute drive to his hotel room. Mark had about a twenty-five minute drive to his destination of Sarah's apartment, but it was easier to get there by blocking through the city.

Mark tried to the ignore the car behind him, and continue on his intended route to Sarah's, but after taking two or three turns with the car still seeming to follow him, he decided to take a detour route. At the next intersection he was supposed to take a left, instead, he turned to the right. The car also took a right turn and stayed behind Mark. Mark took two more out of the way turns and the car was still behind him although it had lengthened its distance a good bit. He could continue to sidetrack the car the whole night, because he had a full tank of gas. By know, Mark had made a complete circle around the block that Sarah's apartment was located. Then, Mark decided to go straight for a few blocks, which he knew would lead him straight past the third precinct of the Mobile Police

Department. However, one block before he passed the precinct, the car turned abruptly at the last stop sign. For now, he was in the clear, but his mind was running circles trying to figure out who was interested in his every move. Once he was sure that the car was no longer tailing him, he made a few more out of the way turns before heading back to the apartment.

There were a few available parking spaces in front of the unit of Sarah's apartment. He quickly pulled up and backed into the first open space. He wanted the car to be parked as if it was headed out just in case he had to leave in a hurry. Also, with it being completely dark outside, the car could give the impression that someone might still be sitting in the driver's seat. After he got out of the car, he quickly jotted up the stairs to apartment B3. He used the spare key that Sarah had given him on the second day he came home after graduating to open the door. He saw no sign of Sarah, but the bathroom door was shut with the smell of soap and shampoo floating in the air so he knew she must be in the shower.

After a short while, Mark started to relax a little, but he still managed to look out of the window for any sign of the vehicle every five to ten minutes. When Sarah was out of the shower, he would tell her all about the suspicious guys that seemed to be keeping track of him, and how the events were beginning to make him very concerned. Maybe someone at the firm would know what to do in a situation where someone was being put under surveillance by who knows who and for no apparent reason besides being young and getting ready to enter law school. He tried not to make being black a part of the dilemma.

Sarah entered the room very refreshed from taking a shower and from seeing her loving boyfriend whom she had been waiting on to come home since she got off of work. Mark was delighted to see her also, but couldn't help but to show a sort of worried look from being followed for the past hour or so. Sarah proceeded to meet Mark at the edge of the bed as if she hadn't noticed a somewhat perplexing facial expression on his youthful brown face.

"Baby someone's been following me since I came home from the bar tonight with Martin," Mark stated with a bit of frustration in his voice. "As of matter of fact, I've been getting followed pretty constantly since I have been home from college," he continued.

"Well, who do you think that it could be," Sarah responded very concerned.

"Harold seems to think that they're a couple of undercover law enforcement agents keeping track of me for whatever reason. The truth is, I made sure I kept my nose clean the entire time I was in college, and wouldn't dare do anything now to jeopardize my future. In three years I plan to have may license to practice law," Mark stated firmly.

Now, Sarah begin to think about asking one of her sources down at the police station to check into any active investigations on Mark Johnson. She decided that she wouldn't mention her relationship with Mark though. With any luck they could pull up something in their files, however she knew that the two men could be federal agents or not police at all. If they were feds, it would be extremely difficult for her to get any information about a possible investigation. On the other hand, if the men weren't cops, she could contact a private investigator to get to the bottom of things.

"Don't worry Mark. I'll check into it. You know I have accumulated a few connections since I've been working at the law office," she stated. You just keep going to work at the office as if nothing is going on until you go to the orientation at Virginia Central Law School. By then, I should know something. If I haven't found out anything by then, it's definitely not the police," she assured him.

Her encouraging words made Mark feel at ease as he lay back on the bed with his hands folded behind his head. He still thought about some other possibilities for the men to be following him. One being the possibility that it was related to the application that he put in for the Marines officer training program. Maybe they were checking on him to see if he qualified to enter their program for officers.

Chapter 4

Harold had been driving for six hours as they entered the city limits of Richmond, Virginia, which was half of the total time it took to get there from Mobile. Mark drove the first six hours, but he agreed to let Harold drive the rest of the way while he got some sleep. The sky was clear almost the entire drive there, but had begun to get dark and cloudy as they exited the interstate to look for a decent hotel room. It was also getting close to sunset, which added on to the darkness of the sky.

Virginia Central Law School, Mark and Harold's reason for coming to Virginia, was located in the city of Richmond. The school was founded in 1958, and had a good reputation for training minorities who wished to pursue a career in law. Mark would attend the orientation for the freshman class of 2030 tomorrow, which was Monday August 8th.

After about thirty minutes of driving through Richmond, Mark and Harold decided to check in at the Motel 6. It was now completely dark and would make it a little harder for anyone tailing them to keep an eye on them, especially, with all the turns that Harold made before settling on the Motel 6.

Harold got out of the car first and entered the office of the hotel to inquire on the availability and price of their double rooms. The desk agent done a quick search on her computer before informing Harold that there were only a few double rooms available and the price would be sixty-nine dollars plus tax. "Would it be possible for me to get a room on the second floor or higher," Harold asked politely. He knew that a higher level room would have a better view for them to watch any suspicious activity in the parking lot.

The desk agent responded, "of course" after a quick glance at her computer screen. Harold was relieved and told the agent that he would be right back to make a payment for a double for one night.

After they were completely checked in into the hotel room, Mark and Harold immediately began getting ready to go out on the town the night before Mark's orientation at Virginia Central Law School. Harold intended to find some hot young lady at the club that he could bring back to share his side of the room, while Mark was just looking to relax a little after the long drive from Mobile. He couldn't stop thinking about Sarah, but decided to wait until the morning to call her. He didn't want to worry her with the idea of him going to a club, especially, since he had told her about being followed recently.

Mark and Harold entered a club called Fortunate a little before eleven o'clock. They were referred to Club Fortunate by some cool looking guys at the gas station near their hotel room who were also headed there for the night. Once they had the name of the popular night spot in Richmond, they simply googled the directions there on Harold's smartphone. Before they went in, the security carefully checked their IDs and patted them down thoroughly. Mark had absolutely no problem with being checked. It made him feel safer, and he wasn't the violent type. Harold, however, would take his pistol to church with him if he could, so he wasn't a fan of security checks at clubs. He felt safer with his own protection rather depending on security to defend him.

The club was thoroughly packed, especially for a Sunday night. There was smoke throughout the club and the lighting appeared to be a cool blue color. As they approached the bar to get the first round of drinks, Harold spotted a group of three women standing near the bar involved in light chatter. All three had on some form of tight dresses, and were holding drinks as they spoke with each other. He paused for a moment to figure out which girl he wanted to run game on while Mark continued casually for the bar. After a moment of contemplation, Harold decided that he would go with his usual choice, the thickest one amongst them.

Meanwhile, Mark's decision making process was focused on which drinks he would be choosing for Harold and himself. The bar had plenty of liquor to choose from, but Mark knew off top he would be getting something light and a beer to go along with it. He knew Harold liked his drinks straight but on ice. After a few seconds, Mark decided on a lime margarita for himself and a bud light on the side. He hollered over to Harold for his choice, and Harold responded, "get me a double shot of vodka and a Heineken beer," as he focused his attention back on the thick young lady.

Harold and his prospective take home date began chatting as if they knew each other. "So what's your name sexy," Harold asked the lady confidently.

The lady smiled for a moment, then responded that her name was "Charlotte."

"Pretty name, do you come to this spot often," Harold inquired. He had to go through the formalities of developing some sort of bond with the woman with a little charming conversation before asking her to leave the club with him.

"Yes, if you consider coming here twice a month often," she responded to Harold's question.

"Well, I'm happy you came here tonight. Would you like anything to drink," Harold asked like a gentleman. Charlotte quickly responded that she would like a daiquiri. Harold headed to the bar to get the daiquiri for the young lady where Mark was just completing the order for their drinks.

"Hey, Mark go keep the ladies company for me while I get my new friend a drink," Harold said slyly as Mark handed him his straight vodka and bottle beer. Mark agreed to engage the ladies in some light chatter, but only for Harold. He certainly didn't want to give the ladies any impression that he wanted anything further. He couldn't even seem to get Sarah off his mind enough to enjoy the presence of the attractive women in the club this night.

It was only a few minutes before Harold was back with the young lady's daiquiri. It was just enough time for Mark to exchange names with the ladies and let them notice that he probably had a girlfriend. Harold and the girl he was after to get in bed with, Charlotte, continued to hit it off while Mark and Charlotte's friend mostly just observed the scene in the club and occasionally said a few words. Everyone also sipped on their drinks until they had finished three rounds of drinks and a few beers.

After they left the club about an hour before close, Harold exchanged phone numbers with Charlotte and got her to agree to meet him at the room after she dropped her friend off at home. Mark just wanted to hit the bed after those drinks at the club had him a little tipsy. He refrained from calling Sarah after deciding that it was too late, and she had to be to work early in the morning. Harold and Charlotte kept up a little noise for about an hour or so then the room was silent for the rest of the night, and Mark was able to get about four hours of good sleep before the orientation the next morning.

~~

The freshman class at Virginia Central Law School was diverse in gender, race, and age. There was a considerable amount of older students, but there were at least a third of the students under twenty six years old. Many of those students were there on scholarships, and would be the fiercest competition for Mark during his three year stint, as law school is a very competitive environment, and younger students are the most competitive. Two thirds of the students were of ethnic backgrounds, and most of those students were African Americans. There were about an equal share of males and females with males slightly outnumbering females. Overall, Mark thought that this was the perfect class with respect to diversity.

The orientation began exactly at eight am sharp, but the lecture hall was packed at least fifteen minutes before. Mark made it there about five minutes till so he had to do a brief survey of the room to find his seat. Harold decided that he would wait in the lobby while frequently checking the parking lot for any suspicious activity, specifically, of anyone that appeared to be following them.

The first speaker was the dean of students, who was also a professor of contract law and litigation. It was a class taken by all students at Virginia Central Law. His name was Professor Wilson. He began by giving a brief introduction to the school's mission and its "rich" history. Mark, who was sitting next to two attractive females, tried his hardest to pay close attention to the lecture while jotting down brief notes in his packet that went along with the orientation. There were several faculty members scheduled to speak for today's program. Most of the speakers were black professors but some were white, and there were about two women speakers for a total of eight speakers. Each speaker was scheduled to speak for about fifteen minutes, making the program at least two hours in length. Harold would be waiting and watching for the entire time of the program.

The next speaker was a woman professor in her early forties. She was of mixed heritage and still looked quite attractive for her age. Her primary subject was torts law, which was another required class for all freshmen at Virginia Central Law School. Mark listened closely to the stunning professor as she further told the students about the expectations of law. She also gave a brief introduction to torts law, which was a rather new subject to Mark.

By the time the fifth speaker was at the podium, Harold had gotten a little impatient, and peaked into the lecture hall only to receive a few agitated stares from the faculty and students. He caught the attention of Mark, who waived him out as soon as he made eye contact. He decided to walk outside for the remainder of the orientation, and had decided that he could wait in the car with the air conditioner blowing. Before he could make it out the door, he bumped into a broad shouldered character wearing a very professional like suit. The guy was wearing prescription glasses, but Harold couldn't help but realize that it was one of the guys that he caught observing them at the employment office.

"Do I know you," Harold asked the guy. He didn't want to get too hostile with the guy, because he still believed the guy was some kind of police officer.

The guy firmly responded, while straightening his tie, " I don't believe you do sir, now excuse me." Harold stepped aside, but was growling under his breath. He had finally exchanged words with one of the creeps trailing his close friend, Mark, and who had began to irritate him personally.

Harold decided to stay in the lobby to see exactly where the guy was going. He observed the guys waistline for any sign of weapon or a badge, but there wasn't any bulge. To his surprise, the guy walked right into the lecture hall where Mark was attending the law school orientation. Harold quickly followed the guy to the lecture hall entrance door, and peeped inside to observe the guy's intention. The guy simply sat in the nearest empty seat designated for the students, but Harold could tell that this man was no student. Harold decided to close the door again after catching eye contact with Mark, and realizing that he had also recognized the creepy figure enter the room.

Mark tried not to ponder too much about who this guy was that had followed him all the way to Virginia from Mobile, and now had taken a seat in the middle of an orientation given for the future law students o f Virginia Central Law school. The man glanced back at Mark for a few seconds as the last speaker for the program was getting ready to step to the podium. Mark tried to look directly at the podium but kept a slight view of the character from the corner of his eye.

The last speaker was none other besides the Dean of Virginia Central Law School. He was known around campus as Dean Mike Baxter. Dean Baxter was a medium height man with a round belly. He was bald on the top of his head with a well trimmed beard and mustache that connected with the little hair that he had along the side of his head. He spoke with a drag, and Mark thought that he would take at least an hour to give a fifteen minute speech. However, he had a short message to give this day. It focused on one of the most important matters for law school students, which was the topic of ethics in the legal profession. With the exception of being a little hooked on placing a good bet on a hot football or basketball game, Mark walked the straight and narrow, so he almost decided to leave before Dean Baxter was finished speaking. He was itching to see if the guy who had been following him since he finished undergraduate school, and who had now followed him all the way to the orientation, would leave if he chose to leave early.

In a few more minutes the dean would be through speaking, Mark thought. He decided to wait it out. He thought, maybe the guy would even introduce himself as being some kind of representative of the school. However, if he turned out to be some maniac thug seeking to recover money from an old gambling debt, Harold would be waiting outside and probably had already retrieved the loaded gun from the car.

Finally, the dean gave his final remarks, and wished the freshman class of Virginia Central Law a prosperous freshman school year. Then, he stepped down from the podium and began shaking the hands of the students as they exited the lecture hall. Mark remained sitting for a while as he waited for the guy who was following him to exit the room. The guy finally got up, and passed the dean without shaking his hand. Mark decided to exit at that point, and gave the dean a nod as he passed. There were several students waiting in line to have a few brief words with him, which persuaded Mark to decide to wait and meet him once the school year started.

Suddenly, Mark felt a rather unwelcomed grip on his right shoulder and almost had begun to remove it when he heard a voice say "Mr. Johnson you don't know me yet, but we have been watching closely. We're not out to hurt you." It was one of the guys who had been following his every move since he had graduated from college. Mark noticed how formal the guy spoke and postured himself. He couldn't help but think this guy is from the military or some other bureaucratic organization.

Mark asked the guy, "who are you and who do you work for."

The guy responded as if he were going to smile, but quickly straightened his expression before saying, "you will know in due time," and walked away just as Harold had walked up to see what was going on.

Chapter 5

Sarah hugged Mr. Cunningham tight and gave him a soft kiss while whispering in his ear that she couldn't wait for the next time to be alone with him. The two had been having somewhat of an affair for the past year while Mark was off at college in Birmingham. Their most frequent gathering was, earlier that week, the Sunday that Mark left to attend the orientation in Virginia. They met in his office this morning to discuss how they would cover their tracks so that Mrs. Cunningham or Mark would never expect that they were intertwined with each other. As she walked out and closed the door to his office, she held her bosses hand gently letting her fingers caress his palm.

Shortly after Sarah left her boss and secret lover's office, Mark was pulling up to the office parking lot. He parked in the spot next to Sarah's car although there was a parking spot available that was closer to the building entrance. He liked the idea of his car being close to his one and only girlfriend's car. It was symbolic of their relationship he thought. Once inside the office, he went directly to the little corner of an office that had been arranged for him the first day he began working for the firm. Sarah was there waiting on him showing her pretty white teeth as she smiled and kissed him on the cheek. He wasn't running late. Sarah had beat him to the office to meet with Mr. Cunningham about their affair, but told him, before he could ask, that she was there early to help get attorney Cunningham prepared for the trial he was expected to attend in Washington County on that morning. Mark had heard a little about the case, and viewed a summary of the case while printing some files for Mr. Cunningham.

"Are you going to assist him in Washington County at the trial," Mark asked.

"No, baby I will be here at the office staying busy with this month caseload here in Mobile." Sarah knew that she didn't want to appear as having the opportunity to spend mutual time with her partner in infidelity.

"Maybe you should go Mark. It would give you a chance to see what the legal profession is really all about, especially, in a rural area of Alabama. You know we do about twenty percent of our cases in surrounding counties," Sarah suggested with no sign of guilt on her face. Mark thought about it for a while, and decided he should assist Mr. Cunningham with the trial. The trial was for a drug distribution of crystal meth case in which the defendant supposedly sold an undercover agent an ounce of high grade meth. The drug cases were always interesting to Mark.

"Yea, baby I guess I will go with him," Mark stated.

"Great, I will let Mr. Cunningham know that you would like to help with the trial," Sarah responded. Sarah left the room with a cunning smile on her face. She had arranged for her secret lover and loving fiancé to spend time with each other in order to make it seem as if there was nothing to hide between her and her boss.

~

The courtroom in Washington County was like the traditional courthouses you see on Perry Mason or Matlock. You could sense the smell of justice floating in the air. Today, Mr. Cunningham was hoping that the wings of justice flew in the direction for him and his Client, Job Macon. Mark was sitting next to Mr. Cunningham observing what the scene of a courthouse was like before court began session. He made sure he put on a nice sport coat with a smashing tie before he left the office.

Mark couldn't help but notice that Job was extremely nervous, which could be a sign that Job was feeling like he would be found guilty at the end of the trial. He hoped the best for the guy, because if he was to be found guilty he could do ten years in the big house. In Washington County it wasn't unusual for the judge to hand down the max sentence to a defendant when he gambled and took a case to trial. This was even more truthful with cases involving crystal meth. Mark knew that

Ice is a pure form of crystal meth, and is highly addictive
and causes addicts to become violent at times. If he
weren't on the side of the defense, he would feel that Job
deserved as much time allowed.

The judge hit the gavel and told everyone to rise as
he spoke the rules of the courthouse to be followed by the
defense and the prosecuting attorneys. The clerk then
swore in the jury, and instructed them to judge the case
fairly according to the evidence presented. The evidence
wasn't that extraordinary, but the State did have the
sworn testimony of a credible police officer on their side.
Both, Mr. Cunningham and Mark could tell that Job was
nervous, because his legs began to tremble as he looked
over to the prosecutor's table. "Have a little faith young
man. I've defended suspects in dozens of drug cases, and
have had pretty good success in most of them ," Mr.
Cunningham spoke to Job in a most encouraging tone.

Mark was observing and admiring how Mr.
Cunningham was handling everything in the courtroom. He
could just see himself being the representation of an
unfortunate young man wrapped up in the street life
against the often cruel and racist organizations of
Southern police departments. He still had no idea that Mr.
Cunningham was screwing the love of his life behind his
back.

The opening statements for the defense and the
district attorney's office would be the first thing to take
place in a criminal trial in Alabama and most other states is

what Mark could remember from the little knowledge he had gained prior to starting law school in the Fall. The DA's office went first while Mark jotted down notes of their key points stressed while presenting their case. They seemed to be relying on the testimony of the officer and the lab results of the tests which determined that the substance was indeed Ice. What the DA lacked was a clear picture or voice recording that would identify their client, Job Macon, as the person who sold to the undercover officer.

Next, Mr. Cunningham stood up and walked around the defense table as he presented the opening statement for the defense to the jury. His opening statement was prepared with the help from Sarah back at the office a few days earlier while Mark was at his law school orientation.

Mark noticed that Job had begun to relax a little as Mr. Cunningham spoke convincingly to the jury about his innocence in the case. This pleased Mark, because Mr. Cunningham told him that the jury would be studying Job's body language for any sign of guilt. Mark had also begun to relax, because he had started to identify with job's situation of being a young black male. And, he couldn't help but think about his friend, Harold, who was also involved with the street life back in Mobile. He thought to himself that this trial could have been for his good friend. He thought of Harold as a good friend because he had a good heart, and he always had his back when he needed him.

Mr. Cunningham concluded his opening statement by saying "My client just happens to be from the rough side of the tracks, but he didn't sell those drugs to that undercover officer that day, and the DA has no proof to indicate that he distributed anything to anybody as you will see as this trial proceeds." After finishing the last statement, Mr. Cunningham took a seat next to Job and Mark. The Judge spoke briefly and asked the prosecution were they ready to call their first witness. The assistant DA stood and told the Judge they would be ready to call the first witness after a short recess. The judge agreed, and instructed everyone to be ready to pursue the trial at 1:00 pm.

The assistant DA was a young white male who had started his current job about two years ago fresh out of law school. Mr. Cunningham was happy to have someone with so little experience as his opponent, but then again, young attorneys were ambitious is what he knew from experience. The young prosecutor would be attempting to convince the jury of Job's guilt to the fullest extent.

The Judge, however, was Judge Aiken, and he had been a judge for eleven years. He was in his late 40's. Judge Aiken had been both a defense attorney and a prosecuting attorney in his time in the legal profession. He had represented clients in Mobile, Montgomery, and Birmingham during his time as a defense attorney, so he was quite familiar with the techniques used by attorneys from the bigger cities such as attorney Cunningham. He had also come from a Christian religious background. His father was in politics, and had aggressively backed a prominent judge in his battles to maintain a traditional sense of ethics in the law profession and in courtrooms. Also, he hated drugs and the sinful nature of the activities that it brought about.

~

At about a quarter after one o'clock, the prosecuting team called their first witness, the lieutenant from the Washington County Drug Unit, who allegedly oversaw the whole operation in which the defendant sold to an undercover officer. His testimony was rather convincing. He confirmed that there was an undercover "buy" by Officer Armstrong on the date and time as stated in the accusation against Job, however, he did admit that it was very difficult to tell if the picture was that of Job Macon. Mark wanted to smile as Mr. Cunningham repeated the Lieutenant's testimony to the Jury. "You really can't tell who that person is in the picture," Mr. Cunningham stated while briefly turning from the state's witness to look at the jury.

There were several other witnesses called by the State before they called their star witness, Officer Armstrong, who gave a less than admirable testimony that he could identify Job as the person who sold him the ounce of pure ice. Basically, he stated that he was "ninety percent sure that the person in the photo was job. What he failed to recognize was that the person in the photo appeared to be clean shaven, but job had sported a full faced beard during the entire year that the photo was taken. This would be a key point to prove Job's innocence when Mr. Cunningham cross- examined Officer Armstrong.

He estimated the street value of the drug to be about two thousand dollars, which was probably on the high end of estimations. Mr. Cunningham knew from previous drug cases that an ounce of ice would probably only be worth about fifteen hundred if sold in one unit. Mark couldn't help but to think that no amount of money was worth doing ten years in the pen for.

The first thing that Mr. Cunningham pointed out in cross examination was the inconsistencies in Officer Armstrong's testimony. There were small areas of concern like why the picture seemed to be taken with little light, although it was supposedly taken around four p.m., which was long before the sun had set that day. Mr. Cunningham pointed out to the jury that "the photos were probably manipulated so that you couldn't say for sure that the person was indeed someone other than my client." Job sat up in his seat with confidence as he had assured Mr. Cunningham that definitely was not him in the photo. Mark didn't know what happened to the photo, but he also believed that the picture didn't show Job selling ice to the undercover. The photo was so dark and blurred that the person in the picture could have been anyone. It could have been anyone with a clean shaven face that is. The lack of facial hair on the person is exactly the point Mr. Cunningham was to make next.

"Officer Armstrong, would you agree that the picture shows a male figure with little or no facial hair," Mr. Cunningham tactically inquired of the State's so called star witness. The witness who's testimony should have proved the case for the Washington County District Attorney's Office. Instead it seemed to be the deciding factor in favor of Job Macon's acquittal. Officer Armstrong grudgingly admitted that "it looks like the picture shows someone with little or no facial hair." "Well, Mr. Armstrong I have pictures entered into evidence that the defendant, my client Job Macon, took on the day of the alleged distribution shortly after the time given by your report as to when the sale took place," Mr. Cunningham spoke with the confidence as if he had witnessed Officer Armstrong create a fraudulent case to put another young black male behind bars.

Mr. Cunningham went to the table for the defense where Mark and Job sat watching the entire scene and grabbed the photos from a manila folder stamped with "defense evidence." First, he showed the photos to the assistant district attorney, who unpleasantly looked on them with disgust as they could see pictures from the social media site, Facebook, showing that Job had a very thick full face beard, and that they were taken immediately after the date of the alleged distribution in which Job was on trial for. Mark knew that those styles of beards were known in the hood as "Rick Ross" beards, although Job's beard on the picture wasn't quite as long as some of the guys who sported that style. However, his beard was still too full on the Facebook picture to have grown in a matter of hours.

Judge Aiken motioned for the pictures to be brought up to the bench so that he could have a look at them. Mr. Cunningham retrieved the pictures from the assistant district attorney, and handed them to Judge. The judge carefully viewed the photos to make sure that they were admissible forms evidence in the trial proceedings. The important part for the defense would be what the jury thought about these undisputable photos. You could clearly see on the Facebook photos that the beard was genuine, and why would he wear a fake beard if he had no idea that he was a suspect in a recent drug distribution were some of the simple factors for the jury to consider.

Before the photos could be shown to the jury for consideration of Job's proof of innocence, the assistant DA asked for a short recess to discuss the contradictory photos and the possibility of negotiating a deal.

On most court television shows the DA's office and the defense team would meet in the judge's chambers to discuss shocking revelations and possible deals, but in Washington County, the prosecuting attorney simply walked over and began discussions at the defense table.

With Job and Mark sitting at the table with open ears, the assistant DA blurted out "five years probation and we will drop the case." Job's facial expression got a little more hopeful, but he was really hoping for the charges to be dropped.

Mr. Cunningham told the assistant DA immediately "absolutely out of the question. I just presented evidence that proves my client's innocence."

"Well, the lowest we will go is to reduce the charges from distribution of methamphetamine ice to plain ol' unlawful distribution, and place your client on unsupervised probation for two years," the assistant DA offered in what seemed to be a deep southern drawl.

While it is not what Job deserved in this case, Mr. Cunningham didn't want to take the chance with the mostly white jury. Many members of the jury probably considered Job guilty before the trial even started, and would probably side with the undercover drug agent.

He consulted with Job for a brief moment, who was thrilled with the new deal to a sentence that didn't include any jail time. He was already convicted of a previous felony in which he served six months when he was nineteen.

"I'll agree to plead guilty for the probation," Job uttered with a little bit of urgency.

"Okay we will take your offer," Mr. Cunningham reluctantly stated to the young prosecutor.

Mark sat back and listened to the whole deal with a bit of confusion. "How could you plead guilty to something that we had good evidence proving that it wasn't you in the picture," Mark questioned Job.

"I couldn't take the chance of being away from my girlfriend and kids you know. And, if I would have gotten completely off, the cops would have been harassing me until they found something to send me to jail for," Job replied.

And, just like that, Mark discovered that the scales of justice weren't always balanced. They were especially unbalanced in the South. After that day, Mark knew it was a lot he had to learn if he was going to be successful in this law thing.

Chapter 6

It had been a long summer for Mark since
graduating from undergraduate school. He first had to

make the transition from Birmingham back to Mobile. Then he had to adjust to living full time with his girlfriend and obtain a temporary job while waiting for law school to begin. While working temporary for the law firm that Sarah worked, he witnessed a trial where a defendant had all but proved his innocence, but plead guilty to probation and was thrilled to receive the sentence. He had to do all this while being followed by people who could be anyone from either goons to federal agents, and was still waiting for them to clarify why they were trailing his every move. The next step in his life would be to start his first year at Virginia Central Law School.

Thus, on his first day of School, Mark walked on campus proudly, knowing that he had a girlfriend, family, and loyal friends to support him while he explored his path through law school. He was somewhat early for his first class of the day, Intro to Torts, and was one of the few students sitting in the lecture hall. He arrived fifteen minutes prior to the start of class with his book and all the other required materials in hand so that he could get a little preview of the first chapter to be covered.

After about ten minutes of reading the material, students began entering the class all enthusiastic about their new journey at Virginia Central Law School. One by one they all took a seat. Some immediately opened their books while others were busy chatting, probably, about the subject of torts law or the study of law in general. Many had worked in jobs related to the field of Law before starting the year like Mark, and were anxious to reveal to their new fellow classmates about their experiences.

As Mark was prepping himself on the course material in the first syllabus, an older woman with long black hair sat in the desk next to him. She was a fairly dark skinned Caucasian lady, and only stood a couple of inches over five feet. Mark estimated her age to be about thirty-nine years old. He assumed that she was either Italian or had some Hispanic in her blood.

"Hi, my name is Gwenda Paseney," she greeted Mark.

"I'm Mark Johnson," he responded.

Mark could tell that she had some objective to pursue by the way she was gesturing when she began the conversation with him. "I'm from Brooklyn, New York," she revealed to Mark with an accent that easily suggested that she was. "I don't believe you're from Virginia yourself are you," she asked Mark politely.

"No, I'm from a little city in Alabama called Mobile," Mark responded. How she knew from only exchanging a few words that he was not from Virginia, Mark could only imagine.

"I know exactly who you are Mr. Johnson. I am a captain from the U.S. Marines, and I have seen your application to join the Marine officer program. I have also seen an extensive file that has been created since you first sent in your application," the lady now known as officer Paseney stated.

At that point, two men in dark suits, walked into the lecture hall and stood at the podium next to the torts law professor. Mark quickly recognized the two figures as the guys who had been trailing him during the summer since he graduated from undergrad school. He shuffled the papers on his desk briefly and closed the torts book so he could try to make sense of it all. He knew that the men could possibly be connected to the law school, but what did they have to do with this mysterious lady who claimed to be an officer with the Marines.

It wasn't long before his curiosity was taken away when Officer Paseney spoke up. "I see that you are familiar with officer Lake and officer Goldy," she stated. Mark nodded his head in agreement while he continued to observe the two men at the podium as they seemed to be setting up for a presentation or something.

"Yes, those men have been tailing my every move for the entire summer. They even followed me to the orientation last month. I thought they may have been some hard hitters for a loan sharp that I done business with while in college. Now you're telling me that they are officers with the Marines like you," Mark stated in an attempt to clarify the situation.

"They're reserve officers in the Marine Corp, but they are active FBI agents. They're part of an elite joint task force between the Marines and the FBI called the 'Falling Angels of America' or 'FAA'," officer Paseney stated quietly.

Officer Lake and officer Goldy are preparing to give you a detailed briefing on all the details, and what it is that they need you to do along with a select number of students in this class."

"Exactly, how much do they know about me and the other students in this class," Mark inquired.

"They know just about everything they need to know about you from the first day of kindergarten up until the time you walked into this classroom today." The other select students have also been researched and followed thoroughly," Paseney stated.

Mark turned his attention to the two men while he waited to see what he had gotten himself into by contacting the Marines to inquire about a career in the military. He had a thousand questions to ask, but he couldn't think of how to ask for the information that he wanted to know. He thought about the name of the elite unit, Falling Angels of America. To him it sounded like some religious group, and it definitely had to be top secret. Hell, almost everything involved with FBI was confidential.

"Will I be able to continue in the law school or will it be like a paid internship in the field of law," Mark decided to ask.

"No and yes", Paseney responded. " I doubt if you will be able to continue in law school until after the job is complete, but there will be a generous amount of pay eventually if you complete the tasks without being killed," she stated while staring him directly in his eyes.

"Woe, I don't think I want to get involved in this job if there's a serious risk of getting killed," Mark reacted. He wanted to join the Marines for the benefits, but hadn't really thought about the risks it could entail. He imagined that he would sit at a desk doing lawyer stuff.

"You did apply to join the Marines Mr. Johnson," Paseney added. She had begun to use his last name as a way of showing that she was being formal and to indicate the seriousness of the proposition.

"Sure I did, but I have not made a final decision, and I certainly did not swear an oath to join the Marines. Do I even have a choice anymore now that your team has devoted so much time to investigating my entire personal life," Mark inquired looking somewhat troubled.

Before Paseney could respond, the torts professor called for everyone's attention as she began to introduce the class to an overview of the course, and to reveal to them what the two agents standing next to him were there to speak with them about.

She stood to the podium and began speaking. "As you know this class is designated to be for "Introduction to Torts," she spoke clearly. "For those of you who have no idea what a tort is in the field of law, I will gladly define it, and further explain to you what this class is all about." Mark began to relax a little, because this first part of the lecture is what he was expecting when he anxiously came to class with his course book and materials.

"Torts are basically civil wrongs committed by one person to another person," the professor began. "The major difference from criminal law is that a tort can be committed by negligence, and is often a civil matter. In this class we will explore the elements of tort law, as well as examine cases of examples that involve tort law versus criminal law," she continued.

"However, today we have some very important guests that are here to discuss a very important and complicated matter. A person with a solid mind interested in a legal career will find this information and opportunity quite interesting, and may choose to explore this option as a step towards getting ahead in a legal career. Given that all of you here have decided to explore a career in law, this opportunity will be unique to your interests although it may not be for everybody in this class. Now I will introduce the class to Officer Lake," the professor stated at the conclusion of her overview of the course and introduction to the guests.

Officer Lake was a thirtyish white male agent who loved his career in the Marines as well as his job with the FBI. He stood about six feet one with traditional glasses and conservative cut dark brown hair. His involvement with the falling angels of America operation had become his life. He would be giving the overview of part one of the operation to be conducted by the selected students of which Mark Johnson was sure to be among those selected.

Lake began his presentation by greeting the class and announcing to them that what they were about to hear was of the highest classified information that the United States government wanted to keep secret. "The material in this presentation is so confidential that I will ask those of you students who will not allow us to electromagnetically erase your current memory of the things talked about today to leave at once," Lake cautiously warned the students.

Mark thought about getting up and leaving immediately. He knew that there was technology around that could erase a certain amount of a person's memory, but he didn't want it practiced on him, and he sure didn't think he wanted to be a part of something so confidential. However, he did want the opportunity to advance his possibilities in the legal field. Maybe he could still get a job as a lawyer in a federal department. He thought about the newscast he seen while in the bar with Martin concerning Attorney General Mills and some revelation of a scientific life changing technology. He knew that this was somehow connected. It was something that he wanted to be a part of so he made the decision stay and listen to the presentation.

Lake walked around the class as he let the information settle in the mind of the students, and to give those who didn't have the guts to stay and hear him out a chance to leave. He particularly glanced frequently at Mark after remembering the occurrences he had while trying to follow him to get a picture o f how he managed on a day to day basis. He admired his ability to get his friend Harold involved with helping him after discovering that he and officer Goldy had been following him. A relative amount of street smarts would be useful with surviving the mission that they were going to send those selected students to do.

"Well the job is primarily focused on investigating the activity of law enforcement agencies in the southern region of the United States," Lake began. "As you now there have been segments of the country that are under the influence of vast corruptive elements. While this corruption occurs across the regions of the United States, our investigation will just focus on the dirty south as it is known. The Federal government has kept a careful watch on the South since before the Civil War, and special units under the control of the NSA and Central Intelligence Agency have even secretly spied on those politicians from the southern states who happen to get elected to federal offices," Lake continued.

Mark's eyes began to become intense as he focused on Officer Lake give very privileged information to some very ordinary first year law students. However, he didn't quite find the information surprising after seeing what and happened to Job Macon at his trial during his stint working for the law firm. Harold had also told him numerous stories of dirty cops in the dirty south. Furthermore his friend, Martin, had told him of some hostilities between army officers from the South and those from the northern military academies.

Lake stopped for a while and glanced out of the window as if he were looking for someone to be spying on the classroom before he abruptly closed every shade curtain in the room. He continued speaking, "Instead of formally investigating these southern police agencies, you will be operating as undercover civilian citizens with contacts to only officer Goldy, officer Paseney, and myself. For the most part you can continue your ordinary lives. You can even have a normal job as long as it is not in any high profile position such as, high level business positions, law enforcement, or anything in the legal field."

Mark thought about those last statements and was somewhat relieved. He would be able to stay in his relationship with Sarah, but he would have to take a break from most legal and professional jobs. He didn't mind. He had worked in several restaurants and retail stores since he turned sixteen. He looked over at Officer Paseney, who was still sitting in the seat next to him, and asked about the pay he could expect while conducting the operation. He would definitely need more money than a part time job to live on, and to help Sarah pay the bills.

Officer Paseney interrupted Officer Lake, "Can you tell the students about the compensation they can expect to receive while participating in this duty."

"There will not be a set pay schedule for those of you who are to operate undercover as ordinary citizens," Lake stated. "Officer Goldy and I will distribute sums of money occasionally to you through unconventional means. However, you are expected to dabble in any illegal activities that you can infiltrate so that you can set yourselves up to be targets of corrupt law officials and other backwards groups. You are allowed to keep any funds you can accumulate from unlawful trades, and the rest of your compensation will be discussed by officer Goldy later in the presentation."

Mark politely asked officer Paseney, "Who are these other backward groups and do I have to break the law to be a part of this thing?"

"These backward groups are part of government programs designed to function as stabilizers within America's communities. There is a whole lot to be covered concerning their role in the current society of America. Exactly how they became uncontrollable by their supervising authorities is a whole different story, and is probably the cause of modern technology breakthroughs," Paseney responded.

"However, officer Lake will gladly inform you about their part of the operation. And yes you are expected to break the law or at least give the impression that you are breaking the law to get the corrupt agencies to feel like they can violate the U.S. constitution to harass, arrest, and possibly commit brutality against you," Paseney added.

Paseney stood up and spoke over the students to officer Lake, "officer Lake could you please tell the students about the vile and mass group of the 'fallen angels' who the chosen students will definitely run across while trying to complete their mission."

"Yes I will officer Paseney," Lake responded. "The fallen angels were a very clandestine group formed in the 1990's to help keep the economy functioning properly, and basically to make sure things happened to keep society as to appear to be a somewhat crooked and violent place as it has always been. They specialized in making headline news stories."

Mark thought about it for a while and remembered hearing something about the 'fallen angels' on an independent documentary, but the story presented them as somewhat of a paranoid conspiracy theory. They distributed money to poor and easily influenced citizens to conduct criminal activity and to create catastrophic events. They also were involved in creating the vibe in pop culture by promoting recording artists and sports figures. Many times those that were promoted would rise to fame only to be doomed to destruction. One example would be the deaths of Tupac Shakur and Biggie Smalls.

"The 90's were a time when the different cultures of America and across the globe had come to a consensus of respecting each other's differences and violent crime was at an all time low in spite of a flourishing drug trade. In other words, everyone was eating," Lake continued with a smile.

"Thus some high ranking republicans in the congress and senate concocted a plan to ruin the legacy of a well liked democratic president at the time whose ratings were through the ceiling. This group they formed, the 'fallen angels', were sort of a reference to devil worshipers themselves, but the name also disguises them as a benevolent organization. Another words, the founders claimed that the name was to imply the meaning of earthly angels," Lake began to get a little intense as he dug deeper into the details of the mission.

"The fallen angels set out to shape society as they felt it should be. They thought it should always be a certain amount of evil in the United States and the world in general. The way they got funded by congress was by suggesting that their evil deeds would lead to a more peaceful and perfect world. The only thing was peaceful outcomes never matured from their deeds. There appeared to be only random acts of devious actions committed in part by the influence of the fallen angels."

Lake shifted towards Mark a little and began to clarify things a little further. "The name of our elite unit is the 'Falling Angels of America.' It was so named to bring attention to the deviant organization of the 'fallen angels', and to remind them that we were here to end their escapade but we were willing to get our hands dirty in the process. Another words, we are falling, but we still haven't fell completely yet, and don't plan on stopping until we no longer have a government entity that suggests such an evil existence."

The remaining students in the classroom were all intensely listening. They had all decided to take the risk of discontinuing their law school pursuit in return for a highly complex job that didn't seem to pay all that much, but the rewards at the end of the job could be endless.

"To make matters worse, the fallen angels were able to get their hands on some state of the art modern technology that allows members of the fallen angels to read the minds of people, and even allows them to control unsuspecting individuals' brains to a certain extent. This technology is in a form of ultraviolet magnetic rays known as "stardust" among those familiar with it."

Lake continued while many of the students looked on with awe. "Once you are assigned to a duty area, you will be fully trained in the use and defense of "stardust."

"Using this stardust substance, the fallen angels have been able to create insurmountable crime in our communities across America. Many of the recent headline news stories are the result of this movement that began with dysfunctional members of our government. It has even been the cause of domestic terrorist attacks in the recent pass, and is further intensified by both federal and local law enforcement agencies. These agencies assist the fallen angels with the denial of rights to those who oppose this corruption."

Officer Lake spoke about the fallen angels with extreme emotion. He was deeply affected by their ubiquitous activities, and had taken many personal losses at the hand of the politicians, corrupt police, and other various members of the vile organization. He wished to pass on his hatred towards the corruption and habitual efforts to control freewill by the fallen angels to his own group of righteous angels, "The Falling angels of America." Under his leadership they would seek to correct every mistake of the fallen angels and to put an end to their secretive but ubiquitous empire.

Lake closed his remarks about the operation to be taken on by the Falling Angels of America by telling them of their arch enemy, the leader of the fallen angels, Attorney General Mills. Attorney General Mills was the de facto head cabinet member over the FBI and the Justice Department. He was also the leader of the hateful group the fallen angels, and the target of the covert operation of Officer Lake, Officer Goldy, and Officer Paseney along with key leaders in the Marines, FBI, and the CIA. The latter group is who controlled the Falling Angels of America. Their goal was to replace Mills, end the use of stardust, and make America a God fearing country again.

"Now, I will hand the microphone off to officer Goldy, and he will instruct you about the second part of the operation," Officer Lake announced to the twenty or so remaining students. However, Mark remained at the forefront of the Officer's attention. For some reason Mark knew that he would play a special role in this operation.

Officer Goldy stood to present to the class the remaining elements of the clandestine operation. He was African American with stout build and intellectual looking glasses on his face. He had been involved in the planning of the Falling Angels of America Program for about ten years. This was during the time that the adversaries to the FAOA, the fallen angels, were busy committing mass atrocities.

"Hello future agents. My name is officer Goldy, and I will fill you in on the expectations of the second part of the operation. In a nutshell, you can expect to do time in jail before the operation is over. Some of you will only spend a couple of days in jail, while others may do months. The remaining agent doing time in the local jail may even do a year or more before we can safely have him released. This agent will be known as the Neutral General of the United States if he survives the stay in jail. We say if he survives, because the fallen angels and corrupt jail officials may try to have him assassinated before the completion of the operation. In fact they are expected to do whatever they can to remain in power. However, we will not fail."

Mark raised his hand and inquired about these new details. "How will we be paid for spending all this time behind bars."

"Good question Mark," Goldy replied. "You will be paid through the awards paid by a lawsuit filed against the local jail for false imprisonment if the jail refuses to release you as they are expected to do. Once you are finally released from jail you will be paid a comfortable salary for your role as the Neutral General. The position is similar to being the president of the United States, but you will play a shadow role to make sure the fallen angels don't continue to operate and to get rid of stardust altogether."

Goldy straightened his glasses and continued to speak. "Furthermore, all of you guys and girls remaining can expect to play a role in the operation. However, only time will tell which of you will actually be involved in an internal affairs style operation involving the false imprisonments. We have other members of the Falling Angels of America who will be assisting you in your duties. Many of these members have been training for a while and have been active agents for years. I wish you all good luck and that you find your way through this mission eventually."

After speaking those last words of encouragement, officer Goldy dismissed Mark and the other students in the class to an unknown adventurous journey.

Part II

The Streets

Chapter 7

Back in Mobile at Sarah's apartment the mood between Sarah and Mark was quite frustrating. Mark was trying to tell Sarah that he would no longer be going to Virginia Central Law School anytime soon. He kept the details of the initiation into a shadow government operation to himself, however, he knew he would have to tell her some details soon or their relationship would be in grave jeopardy. He thought to himself that there would probably be numerous women who he would come in contact with before this thing was over.

"Baby, I just had a change of mind about the whole thing," Mark exclaimed. "You know it takes years sometimes to even pass the bar. What am I supposed to do if I graduate and can't pass the bar exam. He was trying his best not to reveal anything about the presentation that Officer Lake and Officer Goldy had given in Virginia or the real reason that he was home without learning anything about law.

"Is everything ok Mark," Sarah asked." You were so excited about going to law school before you left. Does it have anything to do with those creepy guys who were following you this summer, because I will call down to the district attorney's office and have them taken care of."

"I know baby. Things change, but I will tell you more about it when the time is right," Mark replied sincerely. "Now lets just relax and watch a movie.

Tomorrow I will talk to Martin and Harold about finding a job, because I don't plan on going back to work at the firm." Mark knew the instructions were to either work the streets doing some sort of illegal activity or work some type of low profile menial job. Nothing to tip off the local law enforcement or the fallen angels that he was working for the government.

" Mark why would you want to go out looking for work with Harold," Sarah inquired in a angry tone. "You know his main occupation is selling drugs. He rarely keeps a job longer than a few months."

Mark replied, "That's why he has many contacts for jobs that he worked in the past, and you know I'm not about to sell drugs. I don't know the difference between crack and cocaine." Deep down Mark knew he would probably end up selling drugs before the operation was over. He would need to do time to gain the title of the Neutral General. Officer Lake could fill him in on the basics of dealing drugs and on how exactly he would get the local police to make a false arrest.

"Trust me Sarah everything is going to be A okay," Mark affirmed. " If you would like, you can help me find a job if Martin and Harold are unable to hook me up with something. Remember that I just want to get a break from the stressful field of law and politics for a while. I will eventually get myself back together, and I will be ready to start a family and do all the other good things we were looking forward to."

~

Martin was excited to see Mark for the first time since being discharged from the Army. He had already begun dating women in the local Mobile area to find his true mate so he called it. Life outside the military was an ease he thought. No more strict guidelines on dressing, social activities, or private affairs with women. Mark, however was entering a form of military life where the guidelines were less formal than a normal civilian lifestyle. The Falling Angels of America were strictly about ending police corruption and the influence that the fallen angels had on American society, especially in the South. They cared less about casual affairs with women and drugs or even small time felonious capers.

"Your home soon homie," Martin stated with glad but confused smile.

"Yea, I dropped the law school thing my first day."

"Well, it's still good to see you though. Sorry it didn't work out for you," Martin added while rubbing his chin.

"It's okay though. Some people visiting the school offered me a job as soon as I attended my first class. They basically made me an offer I can't refuse. The job has to do

78

with assisting the federal government right here in Mobile," Mark revealed. He had made up his mind that he could trust his good friend Martin with this information, and he needed someone to confide in if anything went wrong.

"Remember when I told you about the two men following me during the summer," Mark inquired.

"Of course, it had me worried while I was waiting to be released from my duty in the army," Martin replied.

"They were both FBI agents and Marine reserve agents. They are part of an elite joint task unit known as the Falling Angels of America."

"Wow dude, I've heard of them. We weren't allowed to go near that type of classified stuff in the regular army," Martin responded astoundingly.

"Well they have a major operation going on, and I am supposed to be playing a major part in it. I can't tell you too much detail now, but in time, I may be able to let you in on it after I talk with my contacts in the FAOA," Martin spoke quietly with his hands in his pockets and standing if he was a lifelong military man.

"In the mean time I told Sarah that I would try to find a basic job. She doesn't know about my job with the Falling Angels of America or the fact that I may have to do some time soon for something I didn't do to satisfy the requirements of the operation," Mark stated.

"You know of any jobs available that would allow me to keep a low profile," Mark asked.

"Not really. I been solely focused on females and adapting to college," Martin replied. You may want to check with Harold on that. You know he has knowledge of all the openings in menial jobs. He probably could even get you a job with some type of private contractor for a while."

"Of course, the last resort would be to get Harold to set me up selling a little coke or something."

"Are you sure you would want to go that route," Martin asked.

"Yea, I'm supposed to get involved with some criminal activity, because the op requires me to do a little time in the slammer. There's plenty I have to tell you about the operation," Mark explained.

Chapter 8

Washington D.C.

The office of Attorney General Mills was decorated with memorabilia from the time he served in the Marines during the Gulf War back in the early 1990's. His unit was responsible for some of the fierce battles leading up to the surrender of Saddam Hussein. Now, he spent his time overseeing the many controversial legal issues across the United States. Most of the alarming conflicts were initiated by the, fallen angels, the secret group that also operated under his wing of authority.

"There isn't a single thing that I would not do to benefit the country officer Lake," AG Mills stated with what seemed to be sincerity. " I labored hard and risked everything during the Gulf Wars to make sure freedom persevered in America you know. I want to make it better for our kids and grandkids in the future. To ensure that they enjoy all of the benefits that America has to offer has always been my ultimate goal."

Officer Lake listened patiently, however he had watched the injustice that happened under his watch and despised his leadership of the fallen angels. He couldn't understand why Mills allowed it to continue after he rose to the highest hierarchy of the Justice Department, besides the fact that Mills was actually rotten to the core and hungry for power.

"I know you always want the best for the country Attorney General, but the fallen angels are committing more violent acts in the southern states than the general criminal population sir," Lake stated without any expectation of actually influencing Mills to terminate the secretive group that had now become ubiquitous. He thought to himself that his new unit, Falling Angels of America, were in for a difficult task to defeat an organization as huge as the fallen angels. He was sure that AG Mills still was unaware of the coup he planned to enact against the current Justice Department and the country.

"I will hear nothing of the sort officer lake," Mills blasted back at the criticism of his prided creation. "The fallen angels have done many great things for the this country. One of the most important things they have done is winning the election for our current President. They have contributed a whole lot using their mental control of unsuspecting citizens' minds who would have otherwise done unproductive things. I think it was brilliant the way I stationed the fallen angels near the polls during election time, and had them use the stardust to its fullest potential."

Officer Lake decided to agree with Attorney General Mills until he could get the Falling Angels of America agents stationed in every city in the South. "Well, AG Mills, I guess I agree with the things that have been happening in this country lately on behalf of the fallen angels," Lake agreed, but feeling like Mills had become disillusioned with the results of his failed program. Lake also despised the current president that AG Mills had single handedly picked with the technology of using stardust operated by the fallen angels.

Lake knew exactly how the President had gained his office. The process was fairly simple. The agents of the fallen angels surrounded the polling places with stardust that shared the same elements with the star dust in their brain cells through a process similar to osmosis. Once the stardust entered the brains of unsuspecting American voters, the fallen angel agent would meditate certain thoughts which triggered those same thoughts in the voters before they cast their vote. So if the fallen angels wanted President Charles Harding, Charles Harding is who became the President.

"Yes President Harding is an excellent leader sir," Officer Lake continued to agree while waiting to be relieved from the meeting.

"I know you will always do the right thing Lake. I trust you like I trust a favorite nephew or little cousin," Mills stated with the attempt to sway Lake with loyalty.

However, Officer Lake couldn't wait to get back to his new headquarters of the Falling Angels of America in Alabama, and get started with his plans to make the South and the country honorable again.

"If that's all Attorney General, I would like to go and keep doing the good work that you so sincerely applaud, Lake replied."

"Your dismissed officer," Mills stated as he concluded the meeting.

~

Mobile, AL

The alley was still painted with the darkness as Mark awaited the arrival of Officer Lake and Officer

Paseney. They were going to fill him in on the major skills of using the stardust technology, and a few more things that were going to be useful in the operation known as the shadowbox operation. It was called shadowbox for a very good reason. While the fallen angels were already a sort of shadow government entity, the Falling Angels of America would be a shadow agency operating beyond them. In other words Mark and all the other agents from the Virginia Central Law School meeting would be double agents. They would be spying on and sabotaging the agents from the fallen angels that were ran by AG Mills.

After Mark had waited for about a half an hour, two black vans rolled up with tinted windows. For a while Mark was unsure if the vans were driven by Paseney and Lake, because the vans didn't have custom federal license plates. It was necessary that the vehicles that were driven by the Falling Angels of America Unit not to be identified as ordinary government vehicles to escape detection. In addition, they weren't officially on a government assignment.

Mark stepped back about two steps as the doors to the vans opened almost simultaneously. Officer Paseney stepped to him and shook his hand while officer Lake stood closely back and looked cautiously in the direction of the entrance of the alley. Paseney immediately began to speak about their current business.

"There is a good deal to learn about your mission in this region Mark," Paseney began. The directors of the fallen angels have created a web of contacts in the communities across the entire southern region. There are also communities in other regions controlled mostly by the fallen angels. You will be focused on the southern area of Alabama. Our goal is to stop as much of their activity and influence as we can."

"Are there other agents across the country active in the operation," Mark inquired.

"Of course," Paseney stated.

"The main reason we chose Mobile for the focus of the operation is because it has been one of their strongest holds since the government began experimenting with using stardust to influence all areas of society. Thus, America was once the land of the free, but now it has come to be the land of the mentally enslaved."

"When the Falling Angels of America take Mobile at the conclusion of this operation, agents in other parts of the country will make their move to control their territories. We have inside contacts throughout the government that are on our side. Attorney General Mills and his fallen angels have created their share of enemies."

"Well, I guess you will have some protection for me when I'm out in the field," Mark asked."You know I have plans to grow a family with my girlfriend when this is over."

"That's if she sticks with you through the dirty and tough times you will face in the coming months," Lake remarked as if he knew something Mark didn't. What he knew was that Sarah was already on the verge of leaving Mark, and that she had been having an affair with her boss for months.

"But anyway lets get down to business," Lake stated. "The technology of the stardust is quite easy to understand and use. Lets say an unsuspecting individual is in an elevator with you. All you have to do is inhale some of the stardust from a cloth material such as a facecloth. Then, you blow the stardust in the vicinity of the individual's breathing area. Once the stardust is in the individual's system, you can basically control the person's thinking by concentrating on a thought in your own mind."

"Is it really that easy," Mark replied.

"There is one catch though," officer Paseney added. The person cannot figure out that his thought process is being tampered with. If he or she does, they will attempt to fight the temptation to follow their first thought, and will wait until a more rational thought pattern occurs.

"Okay, I can see the potential harm this stardust stuff can cause and create," Mark thought out loud.

"Indeed Mr. Mark Johnson, they trigger thoughts in young individuals all the time to partake in criminal activity such as drugs, robbing, thefts, and even murder", Lake explained to Mark in a tone sounding like a documentary. The thing we need you to do is to clear these individuals' thoughts of negativity by injecting stardust from the thoughts in your brain into the atmosphere that they will be breathing. The agents from the fallen angels will never know, because once they attempt to trigger sparks of thoughts on the victims, they leave it up to the victims to expand those thoughts on their own. And, they always do. You know people choose to do evil if they keep evil thoughts on their mind.

"When you inject more sensible and righteous thoughts, the individual will go back to thinking on a more lawful basis. The fallen angel agents will have to do a lot more work to sabotage the individual's life. This is why we must also stop the network of corrupt law enforcement officials that are knowingly arresting innocent people to keep the cycle of lifetime criminals going. They too are creating a web of crime through blackmail and bribery," Paseney extenuated.

"Well that's enough for today Mark," Lake concluded.

"I advise you to talk with your friend Harold about purchasing some drugs for sale, and setting you up on a corner. The fallen angels are destined to be around somewhere when you start hanging in the streets. Just watch for anyone talking about pulling some news making event, and take the stardust from the rag in your pocket and blow it around them and start meditating on changing that person's mind."

After filling Mark in on how to generally get started on executing his mission, officer Lake and Paseney jumped in their discreet jeeps and headed out of the alley.

Chapter 9

"No way homey," Harold declared. "You want me to hook you up with a package of crack cocaine and a pound of marijuana."

"It's hard times dude is all I can say," Mark replied. He didn't want to fill in Harold on the details of the operation unless he found himself in a tough situation in which he couldn't get out of like if he ended up in the slammer with no bond. He thought hopefully Martin would not disclose any of the details he told him about the identity of the agents who had followed him and Harold at the orientation.

"Just a couple of weeks ago you were going to law school with plans on becoming a big time lawyer Mark. Does this have anything to do with those guys that had been following you this summer," Harold asked.

"Maybe"

"I knew they were cops. You must have gotten yourself in some really big trouble, and they want you to bust someone for them. I'm not setting you up to squeal on anyone. You can get killed out here in these streets trying to do that," Harold spoke to Mark as any caring friend would to protect him.

"No, I'm not trying to rat on anyone. I just need to make some extra dough you know. I believe I can make more money out here than I can at a regular job or in law school." Mark hadn't thought of a good story to tell Harold when he planned to join him in his street occupation, but he knew he could get him to go along with it. Harold was down for almost anything.

"Well I have like a half ounce of hard that I can front you to get you started now." Harold pulled out a plastic bag with something that resembled a half of a peanut butter cookie, and handed to Mark delicately. " It's worth a cool six hundred dollars to me. You can expect to make about that much from it too. You were pretty good at math in school so it shouldn't be a problem breaking it down. Just cut it with a razor into twelve equal pieces, then, cut those pieces into five equal pieces. The pieces you end up with are called twenties." Harold spoke with the mannerism of a high school teacher, but with a sort of clever street slang.

While they were talking, a middle aged guy walked through the door. He slightly taller than Mark and had snag in his teeth right next to silver crown. He wore torn and dingy looking clothing, and walked right up to Harold and asked for two twenties, the unit of the pieces that Mark had just started to cut.

Harold spoke up loudly in a rash voice, "Yo, my partner got you on this one."

"Go ahead and give him two twenties Mark," Harold muttered still not believing that his schoolboy friend was selling drugs with him.

Mark picked up two small pieces from the table and nervously gave them to the drug addict. He wasn't too afraid, because he knew that Harold had his strap on him at times like this and officer Lake, officer Paseney, or officer Goldy was probably somewhere close in case anything went haywire before he could attract the attention of local law enforcement. He didn't want the locals to help him in a dire situation, but he did want them to make a move for a false arrest on him so that he could complete the mission successfully. Officer Lake and Goldy were sure that the locals would make their move sooner or later.

"Man this stuff looks better than anything that I ever got from you Harold," the man stated with a wide grin. "I need to start dealing with your buddy here more often. What's your name guy?"

Mark welcomed this opportunity to get himself some name recognition in his temporary street trade. "You can call me milkman," Mark replied before he could think about it. "You can remember it by the grade of the product I keep all the time. It's just like butter from the dairy."

Both Mark and Harold liked the sound of it. "Yea we gonna call you milkman when you're out here with me," Harold added with an approving grin.

The seemingly satisfied crack addict exited the apartment building with an extra pep in his step as Mark and Harold continued to talk about Mark's new lifestyle. He agreed to hang in the streets and sale these drugs strictly for the sake of the operation. After hanging for a little while, he would return home to his loving fiancé and live like a normal young family man.

Maybe, he had to be in the streets for a while, but he couldn't help but think the sooner he infiltrated the fallen angels and the corrupt legal system in Mobile, the better, and only who knew what Harold would think when he found out that he was an informant for the very same people that were tailing him for the entire summer. Harold was even smart enough to figure out then that they were some type of law enforcement agents while he didn't have a clue about who they were. Sarah wasn't even able to figure out exactly if the men were cops, and she had a ton of resources to tap for the information. If he was lucky, Harold or Sarah would not really know until after the mission was over why he had changed since coming back home from that first day of law school.

~

After making it to Sarah's apartment after his first day hustling with Harold and stopping by the grocery store to pick up a few things with his hard earned drug money, Harold sat watching CNN in a hope to see something concerning the current dealings of the White House. He was really hoping to see any interviews with AG Mills or other officials of the Justice Department. He thought maybe he could decipher some signs of possible corrupt dealings in the Department, and it was a great way to keep his mind from wondering why Sarah hadn't made it home yet. It was past ten pm, and she usually made it by eight thirty when she stopped by the gym and six thirty when she came straight home. Mark had begun to feel that she was slipping away from him to be with another man, but he had no idea it was attorney Cunningham.

A few hours passed with Mark switching between the cable news networks, and he still had not seen anything to indicate that the fallen angels were busy creating havoc on the southern region of the United States. There seemed to be the same amount of crime as it has always been Mark thought. Then he remembered what officer Lake mentioned about the fallen angels involvement with television and music entertainment. He assumed that they probably also interfered with the production of news. Only the news they wished to display was presented in a broadcast to sway public opinion how and when they chose.

Mark turned to MSNBC , and let it stay for a while as he went to the kitchen to try and call Sarah from the house phone since she had failed to answer when he called from his cellular phone. Once again the phone went straight to her voicemail with a simple irritating message, " You have reached Sarah, leave a message, and I will call you back as soon as possible." He began to give up waiting on Sarah, and decided to head to the bedroom at about one am when he heard the door lock turn, and the door creaked open slowly.

Sarah entered the apartment, said, "hey baby" to Mark, and went straight to the bathroom to try to take a shower. The first thing that caught Mark's attention was the smell of fresh Chanel perfume. It was the perfume that he bought her for her birthday this year. He wondered was she showered with perfume to cover up the scent of another man's body fragrances. Before Mark could get his thoughts together, he immediately stopped her before she could shut the bathroom door and pulled her back into the living room.

He gripped both of her arms tightly, looked into her eyes, and angrily asked, "Are you cheating on me Sarah." This was the fiercest action that Sarah had ever seen Mark behave. He was normally very calm and sometimes a bit humorous, but he certainly never displayed actions like he wanted to strike her. Deep down she knew she probably deserved to be at least slapped.

"No I haven't cheated on you Mark," she replied very quickly. "Not tonight," she muttered on.

"Not tonight. What the hell does that suppose to mean," Mark yelled.

"Well, it hasn't been working out for us Mark since you left law school in Virginia. You completely changed your mind about what you want to do with your life. First it was law school now it's any kind of job to get by, and fooling with your friend, Harold, you will probably be selling drugs or pimping women before long."

Sarah sounded disgusted with the possibility that he would pimp women for money, but in her own devious way she was pimping herself to Mr. Cunningham for the various luxury gifts he would buy her.

"Baby, there is so much that I can't tell you right now, but as my future wife you are supposed to be there for me for better or worse," Mark responded in an effort to save his loving relationship with the only woman he ever really intimately loved.

Sarah was having an affair behind Mark's back, but she had no plans whatsoever to end their relationship. Mr. Cunningham was far too old for her to try and raise a family with. She only wanted his money, but she could not tolerate being with Mark if he wasn't going to be successful.

"It's over Mark. You can stay tonight, but I want you to pack your belongings in the morning and leave," Sarah stated with only a single tear in her eyes.

Mark wasn't shedding a tear, but he was hurt terribly and a little bit frustrated with the shadowbox operation, which had now destroyed his relationship with Sarah.

"You're going to regret leaving me Sarah one day," Mark spoke to preserve his pride. "I have more up my sleeve than you could even imagine. And, finding someone to replace you will not be very difficult."

"I'll be back tomorrow to get my things. I don't want to stay around you another night knowing that you've been with another man who has obviously turned you against me." After getting in the last words, Mark slammed the door and left.

Chapter 10

It had been almost three days without a word from Sarah, so Mark decided to get out a little bit and try to meet someone to fill the void. The hustling he was doing for a front was beginning to pay fairly well, and allowed him to get a fresh wardrobe and waste a little money with his new formed habit of drinking. His drinking spot for the night was a bar in middle of town that he heard about from time to time, but had never thought about going. It just wasn't his cup of tea while in college. He didn't bother to get Martin or Harold to meet him there, because he decided that he needed some time to think to himself and revaluate his commitment to the Falling Angels of America. Also, he was hoping he would meet a nice woman to keep him company.

He stepped to a table with two chairs surrounding it and pulled one out to take a seat. His hope was that some fine young lady decided to come to the bar alone, and looking for companionship, would have a seat in the vacant chair.

Tonight was amateur Thursday night on which local artists who wanted to become known performed just for the exposure. Maybe some producer or other professional with connections in the entertainment industry would be there and make them the next Usher or Beyonce.

At the time that Mark walked in there was a duo rap group performing to a platinum selling rap group instrumental known as *The Posse*. The crowd in the bar was mediocre and their response to the performance was pretty much the same. The next performer was a stunning female solo amateur artist whose voice was almost as remarkable as her appearance to Mark. She sang a song that Mark had never heard before. It was song to a mello beat, and the hook went, "I met you on this night, this night, this night. He decided to move a little closer to the stage so that he could try to get her attention. If given a chance, he would call her name, which he had already memorized. He kept repeating it in his head, *Simona, Simona, Simona*.

Simona sang three quick songs in a continuing fashion as many performers did at the bar's concerts. All three songs may have lasted about nine minutes all together, and Mark enjoyed every bit of it. As she left the stage she caught an intense eye contact with Mark, who was sitting at the table staring back at her intensely. He whispered her name aloud before she disappeared behind the stage.

Mark knew that it would be worth him waiting for her to come from the private room behind the stage of the bar if he wanted to have a chance to meet this talented and wonderful young lady. She appeared to be very close to twenty or twenty one, which was within Mark's age range for a suitable spouse. Also, it appeared that she liked being the center of public attention. This could be helpful if he finished the operation and became the neutral general of the United States. Since the position would be a high ranking political office and would probably even replace the U.S. President as the highest ranking office of authority, his significant other would be subject to media speculation also.

About twenty minutes passed before Mark saw her come from the back room and walked to the bar to greet the bartender and ask him for a drink that was most likely on the house. She was clearly an asset to this establishment the way she performed those songs this night Mark thought.

While Mark was observing Simona sip her drink and groove to the music, two young ladies walked up to his table and introduced themselves. "Hi, I'm Gena and this is Tiketa," the obviously more outgoing Gena spoke. Mark thought they were nice young women although he didn't know which one was really interested, but it didn't matter to him at the time. He had to throw them a curve ball before he messed up his chance to meet Simona, who was now beginning to glance at him as he talked to the two women.

"Hi, my name is Mark and I really would like to get to know you girls, but my date is expected to pop up anytime now," Mark quickly came up with a story to turn the young ladies' attempt at starting a conversation down.

The ladies took the objection well, and told Mark that it was nice to meet him as they continued to the other side of the room.

Mark noticed two guys arguing like they were ready to kill one another about two seats down from Simona. Behind the guys were two young men with their backs turned who appeared to be angrily meditating. Mark quickly recognized that the scenario may be his first experience with the actions of the fallen angels who were one of the primary targets of the shadowbox operation.

It looked as if the meditating men were engaging in the mind control techniques that Officer Lake, Paseney, and Goldy had warned him about. They were controlling the two men who were to the point of killing one another. He thought fast on how he was taught to handle the situation. Officer Lake told him to just get close to the person whose mind appeared to be controlled and suck in the stardust from around his breathing air. He had to make a move soon before it went any further, but it had to be done discreetly.

He decided to walk by the men and sneakily inhale deeply while he walked passed them on his designated plan to talk to Simona who had stepped a good bit back from the bar, and was attempting to get her things together to leave the bar before anyone began actually fighting or maybe even shooting.

By the time that Mark got close to Simona, she was putting her purse on her shoulder, and was staring Mark directly in the eyes. The two men who were arguing immediately began to lower their voice, and appeared to be somewhat confused about their hostile behavior, because Mark had skillfully inhaled and discharged all of the stardust that was being used to make them angry. He would report the incident to officer Lake the next day before he went to his cover job of selling cocaine, but now he was going to see what this Simona woman was all about.

"Hi, Simona your performance tonight was outstanding," Mark uttered with a slight feeling of confidence.

"Thanks, and who are you if I may ask," Simona responded. She was curious about Mark, but she sort of knew that he was aware of the stardust that had influenced the two guys arguing in the bar. She too was undercover for the Falling Angels of America.

"My name is Mark Johnson. I came here not knowing what to expect, but once I saw you on stage, I couldn't think of a better place for me to spend the evening," Mark exclaimed in an attempt to let her know that he wanted her deeply.

"Well, I am grateful to meet you too Mr. Johnson. I have been a regular performer at this spot for a few years now," Simona revealed. "I am originally from a town outside of New Orleans, Louisiana, but I have many contacts throughout the Southeast, including Mobile," she added.

At that time a very special song for Mark began to play from the speakers spread around the bar. It was a melody about loving until the end of time. It seemed to be quite appropriate for Mark, knowing what he knew about the fallen angels attempt to ruin the country and possibly the world if the operation couldn't put a stop to Attorney General Mill's plot to destroy freedom.

Simona and Mark came together and began to slowly groove to the song while Sarah contemplated on telling him about her involvement with the operation. She figured he hadn't been in the fight long since she had never heard of him and he appeared to be nervous when he encountered the two stardust controlled men.

After the song came to its last notes, Mark grabbed Simona by the hand, and asked her smoothly could he walk her to her car. "Well James, the head security guard, usually performs that duty, but I guess I can make an exception," Simona responded delightedly. She looked over at James and signaled to him that she would be leaving with Mark. James grudgingly said "okay be safe." He took the duty of walking Simona to her after a show with much pride, but tonight it was Mark's pleasure.

Chapter 11

The corner of Fifth and Lennox was a bit calm today. A few guys were on the side of the package store shooting dice for five dollars a roll with a pocket full of crack. Mark and Harold were on the other side of the street waiting for customers although Mark didn't have any drugs on him. Officer Lake had notified him that there may be a raid today by the local police precinct. He wanted to see what they would do to Mark once they discovered that he didn't have any illegal drugs on him. Lake had also instructed him not to run or resist being pat down.

Mark was a little exhausted of pretending to be a street hustler, but he wasn't ready for the false imprisonment that he was destined for before the mission was complete. He had seen with his own eyes that the stardust was being used by citizens who were more than likely partakers of the Fallen Angels society. Now, he would get a chance to see how the society along with the police was entrapping young lower class Black and Latino males.

"Harold you know me and Sarah broke up the other day right," Mark inquired of Harold who was counting about fifteen twenty dollar bills at the time.

"No, that's bad news man. Did you catch her cheating on you with some lame guy," Harold asked as he counted the last twenty and put the money in his right pocket.

"I suspect so, but she wanted the big life before I could finish getting my business in order. Plus, she had begun to believe I was doing illegal things," Mark answered. "However, I met this fly lady at the bar the other night, and we connected like something in a romance novel. Her name is Simona. You wouldn't happen to know her would you," Mark asked hoping to hear Harold say no. He didn't want the chance of hearing anything bad about her like she was a freak.

"Of course not, but I know that she sings at the bar some nights. The security guards protect her like she's a hidden jewel," Harold added. "She is quite a catch for a guy without a job and just getting his feet wet out here in the streets."

Mark deeply wanted to tell Harold about the mission he was part of, and which he now had Harold in the mist of. A cop passed by slowly, but no one moved. Only Harold and Mark remained on their side of the corner across from the store. Without thinking very hard, Mark decided to tell Harold to get lost, and that he would get up with him tomorrow. He knew Harold was loaded with cash, drugs, and a thirty eight revolver. Harold hesitated before asking Mark "what's wrong."

"It has to do with those officers following me this summer. I can't explain much, but something is going down here today," Mark uttered.

"Whatever you say Mark," Harold replied. "You're the one connected with the legal stuff," he added and then walked quickly out of sight.

Mark knew that he would probably be at least questioned and most likely searched by the police if they were to stop, but he was not sure if they would take the bait and try to plant drugs on him. If they did, Officer Lake and Officer Gordon would proceed with the process to try and bail him out if the jail authorities allowed them to do so, but if they refused, he would sit there and have to sue the county for his freedom upon which he would receive tons of money and a position of supreme clandestine power. This shadow power would be known as the Neutral General of America.

As Mark held a menthol cigarette up to his lips getting ready to light it with a lighter, an unmarked car with a blue light in the center of the dash rolled up and stomped on the breaks directly in front of Mark's sneakers. The two police officers got out of the car with a real devilish grin and motioned for Mark to come to them. These two cops didn't look or act anything like officers from the secret organization that Mark was working for. Mark didn't show any signs of nervousness before he walked up to the officers with his eyes looking directly at them for a short moment. He didn't won't to show any sign of aggression, but he didn't want them to think he had something to hide.

"What's your name," the pot bellied officer asked. "Do you have any Identification on you," he continued.

"Mark Johnson," Mark replied while handing him his old college ID.

Little did Mark know, the officer was already tipped off about Mark and his sudden transition from law school to hanging in the streets. He and his partner, officer Moley, was suspicious of his business here in their precinct. And they both were affiliated with the fallen angels.

"You know we have to search you," the fat officer said. Officer Moley instructed Mark to get against the car.

Mark was quite calm and anticipating for the officers to plant some drugs on him or find some other lame excuse to haul him downtown on false charges. The officers patted Mark down for about five minutes while roughing him up slightly, but nothing to make a case about.

"Well, you're clean fellow," officer Moley uttered and looked over at the other officer with an unsatisfied expression.

Mark was a bit surprised, but he knew this was just the beginning of his troubles with the local police. They were still being controlled by Attorney General Mills and the fallen angels. The officers, looking like they had something up, told Mark to get lost. After Mark made it about a half block away, officer Moley held up Mark's college ID and hollered "Mr. Johnson you forgot your ID." Mark very cautiously headed back in the direction of the officers only to be met by swinging police night sticks. The officers hit Mark repeatedly with their night sticks and threw Mark to the ground where they continued by kicking him in his ribs.

When the officers left, Mark was in and out of consciousness and no one seemed to want to help or get involved. He knew officer Lake and Goldy could not come to his aid immediately, but they were sure to send help or maybe Harold would be back to check on him. He felt hard thumping on the right side of his head before going completely blank.

Chapter 12

The nurse stood by the bed wrapping the last roll of bandages around Mark's bruised head. In the room were Martin and Harold pacing by the bed trying to get the rundown on what had happened to Mark only minutes after Harold departed from him. Mark was conscious, but wasn't talking very clearly, because of the pain to his head and ribs. He had hoped to see Simona today before he was brutalized by the cops and hospitalized for a day. He had her number, and couldn't wait until he was released so he could call her.

Harold was the first to speak to Mark after he came to the hospital in an ambulance. Some of his younger homies had seen the police kicking Mark on the ground, and immediately called him to let him know about his good friend. He sort of felt guilty after remembering that Mark had warned him that something was about to go down with the local cops. He deeply wished he had followed his first mind to stash his drugs and watch Mark from a nearby corner.

"Damn Mark did those crooked pigs do this to you," Harold asked with his hands on his hip and a frustrated expression on his face.

"Who else do you think," Mark mumbled. " I barely remember because of the concussion, but I do recall vaguely that they asked me to come retrieve my college ID, and then I felt the impact of something hard as steel hitting me on the side of my cranium. That was followed by hard steel toe boots ramming into both sides of my ribs. It was the scariest thing I ever experienced. I thought that I was going to die before putting an end to any of the corruption going on in our country."

"Corruption going on in our country," Harold inquired. "Are you still tripping from the head injuries and pain medication they been giving you?"

"Could you please fill Harold in on what's going on," Mark asked Martin while straining to get his words out. The pain killers had not kicked in fully so he was still under a lot of painful stress.

"If you think I should," Martin responded. "All I know is that Mark is part of an undercover operation targeting crooked law enforcement in the Southeast, and now I guess it extends to other parts of the country. It began at the law school in Virginia when he finally met those creepy guys following him this past summer."

"So they were like recruiting you from the law school," Harold asked like it was beginning to make sense to him.

"Exactly, and there is a whole lot of more stuff that I can't tell you about until the mission is near completion and the people who are directing the mission are comfortable with me discussing it. Which it means that it is a certainty that we are going to accomplish all the tasks we set out to accomplish," Mark answered.

"And, what is it that you are trying to accomplish," Harold asked with Martin sitting by waiting to hear the answer himself. Harold wasn't familiar with government operations, and he sure didn't know what a covert operation within the government consisted of.

"Well we're trying to make sure that all citizens are free to use their own mind and that the equal rights of citizens, particularly in the South, are protected by the federal and local governments," Mark explained while still feeling the pain of his injuries. "There is basically a system right here in Alabama where individuals are coerced to do terrible unlawful things then persecuted for them by a crooked and racist legal system."

"It's true Harold. The government has released a substance called stardust to some affiliates that allows the individuals to control the minds of unsuspecting individuals. I know a lot about it from my time in the army. It was supposed to do the opposite by reducing crime in bad neighborhoods, but the crime rate has increased in Black and Hispanic neighborhoods," Martin added.

"The stuff is so major it goes beyond the ghetto into international affairs, but I am only on a mission to save the hood for the time being," Mark stated.

Harold sat by the hospital bed looking at his phone as he received a text message from a customer who wanted some cocaine, but he failed to answer after hearing what Mark was just telling him about the tilted system. He always felt that he was using his own mind to be in the streets, but knew that it was something true about Mark's words.

Harold thought for a minute. "You know those guys who slang on the corner with me can be chilling and everything seems cool, and then before you know it they are either killing each other are trying their best to. And, there always be some weird people around watching like they are spectators. Do you think that has something to do with that mind control stuff you're talking about, Harold asked.

"More than likely," Mark responded.

Mark, Harold, and Martin turned and looked toward the door as it opened slowly. A young gorgeous lady walked in with shades on and a scarf around her neck. The guys didn't recognize her, but they knew she couldn't be a nurse dressed like she was. The room grew completely silent for a moment without anyone making a sound. The lady opened the door slightly again and looked out through the opening as if she was expecting someone to be following her. She sat down in a chair next to Mark's hospital bed and began taking her shades and scarf off.

After squinting his eyes a little to clear his vision a big smile appeared across Mark's bruised face. It was Simona from the bar a few nights before. Mark was hoping to see her again, but he had no idea how she found him in the hospital. He sure didn't want her to think that he was a

114

common drug dealer, or had done anything to deserve being beat up.

She grabbed him by his hand gently as Harold and Martin gestured to Mark that they would be outside the room getting a cup of coffee. "Simona, I am so happy to see you that you wouldn't believe it," Mark uttered trying to sound as clear as possible.

"I feel the same way about you Mark, although I am not surprised that you are in the hospital," Simona responded to a somewhat confused Mark Johnson. She continued talking. It is something I need to tell you. I wanted to tell you this the other night at the bar when those two men were getting ready to fight each other, but I wasn't sure if it was the right thing to do."

"I think I should be able to handle anything you have to tell me at this point," Mark stated. "You know I've been through a lot and am probably going to go through a lot more in the near future."

"I know what you did at the club the other night to make those two maniacs calm down," she began as if she was relieving some deeply held stress.

"How could you? Are you a fallen angel," Mark asked beginning to get disappointed if she was affiliated with the enemy.

"I used to be a fallen angel until I met these cops named officer Lake and officer Goldy. They are the ones who notified me that you had been beaten by the cops and was in the hospital for what they believed would be a short period of time. I've been a part of the Falling Angels of America before you were inducted into the operation." Simona spoke as if it were some fairytale.

Officer Lake and Goldy had arranged for her to accompany the agent who would become the Neutral General of the United States at the conclusion of the shadowbox operation. And at this point, it looked like Mark Johnson would be the lucky candidate.

"I'm like your appointed princess," she continued. "They wanted the Neutral General to have all the rewards of a true king like a beautiful wife, plenty of money, and power. The power would be checked by a committee of representatives in each state who have passed an extensive integrity test. There is freedom of religion, but Christianity has the upper hand because it most exemplifies the natural virtue of humanity."

"This is amazing," Mark exclaimed. "I was beginning to have doubts about completing the mission but you have heightened my enthusiasm. It was just about the cause of saving the country from destruction, but if I get to be with a woman like you, I will definitely go through with it."

Mark was filled with excitement once again, but thought for a moment that it may be unfair to Simona.

"However, I only want you to be with me if you desire to be," Mark added.

"I'm sure I would love to be your companion," Simona responded. "It was like divine intervention that we met each other by chance at the club before you even became the Neutral General. And, if anything happens to prevent you from completing the mission and assuming your leadership position, I will stay with you anyways. Lake and Goldy will just have to find them another princess diva."

"This incident with the police and the fallen angels have made me want to get rid of this system in Mobile and other southern states even more than before, so I definitely plan to do all I can to make the mission successful," Mark spoke with enthusiasm in his voice as if the injuries were beginning to fade.

The door creaked open, and Martin and Harold entered with good news from the nurse saying that he would check out in about an hour after the results from the x- rays came in. Now, Mark had to figure out what he would do until he was healed enough to go back to his undercover activities. He could stay with Martin, but Martin's history in the military might trigger suspicion that he was working for a government agency. Harold's place was too wild with an argumentative girlfriend and plenty kids roaming around.

That only left the option of staying with Simona or his mom, but Simona was not supposed to get acquainted with him until he was through with his potential jail stay and out as America's first Neutral General of the United States. So, he decided to tell the guys to take him to his mom's once he was released from the hospital.

"I'm going to stay at my mom's house for a while Simona until I heal a little more," Mark stated. "I need to talk to officer Lake soon as possible also."

"He has already arranged a meeting for you with officer Goldy, and officer Paseney in a few days. He figured by then the swelling in your eyes would have gone down enough for you to talk about the future plans of the operation," Simona responded.

"Good, I will come to the club to see you perform as soon as I'm back on my feet. I promise," Mark assured Simona while gently rubbing her hand.

Simona grabbed the scarf from the bed and wrapped it around her neck. Then she put it up to her mouth and inhaled as if she was trying to smell the scarf for a fragrance. After inhaling the scarf deeply, Simona blew towards Mark's nostrils and exhaled for a short while. Mark felt the warmest caring feeling he had ever felt. Simona had blown stardust into Mark's nostrils so that he could feel how she was feeling about him. She removed her hand from his hand and placed her hand on her chest and told him "This is how I feel for you at this moment."

Chapter 13

Pensacola, Florida is about sixty miles from Mobile and roughly the same size. There was a little less corruption in the city and even less racism. This is probably the reason that officer Lake and the crew decided to meet Mark there to discuss the recent unplanned police brutality that Mark had suffered and to discuss where to go from there. They met in a small café at the outer limits of town. Officer Lake used to frequent the place when he was stationed at the Pensacola Navy base. He said they had the best coffee in the city besides Starbucks.

Mark walked in with a bruised but healing face and took a seat next to officer Paseney at a booth located at the very rear of the café next to the restrooms. Officer Paseney and Goldy looked at Mark's bruises and sort of felt embarrassed. The only thing that was supposed to result from the operation was a little incarceration. The assault took them by complete surprise. Maybe the local corrupt cops felt as something was up and wanted to send whoever was behind it a message. Either way, Mark endured a lot of pain and suffering.

"We are extremely sorry for what happened to you Mark," Officer Paseney stated with sincerity in her voice. She was old enough to be Mark's mom and had two sons of her own that she rarely seen because of her job, making it difficult to see someone her son's age in such a condition. They basically stayed with their dad most of the time while Paseney travelled the country for her regular job and her covert job with the Falling Angels of America. Each occupation took about forty percent of her time.

"We have uncovered what went wrong during the altercation with the police last week," Officer Lake rushed to explain. "The police officer who attacked you was under the control of a nearby fallen angel member. He was a corrupt officer who normally just harassed the local youth or hauled them in on prompt up charges, but he's only had one accusation of police brutality against him in his fifteen years on the police force."

"Do you think it was his partner?" Mark asked. "He seemed to be a rookie about the same age as most of these fallen angels."

"We're not sure," Officer Goldy said. "According to our inside contacts at the MPD, officer Moley was going to give you back your identification, and then he just snapped like you had really done something to piss him off. The younger officer wanted to beat you up when they didn't find any drugs on you. We know this because officer Moldy revealed it to our inside informant in a casual conversation."

Mark thought to himself that it would have been good to have a comrade from the Falling Angels of America to counterattack the officer with some of their own stardust and mind control techniques during the confrontation. The FAOA agent could have blown the stardust in the vicinity of officer Moley, and he would have been patting Mark on his back instead of hitting him with baton across his head.

"Do you guys think that I should file a civil complaint against the Mobile Police Department for police brutality," Mark inquired. I could request monetary damages in the complaint in addition to asking for corrective procedures to be taken in the local police department."

"You wouldn't win under the current circumstances," officer Paseney stated. "The locals are so corrupt and bent on controlling the world like a game of computer chess with the stardust that Attorney General Mills is underhandedly providing them that they would dismiss any case as such as yours at the preliminary hearing. However, we are working hard in Washington to set up a favorable system within the federal courthouses across the country."

There were many political leaders and judges in other parts of the country that disliked Attorney General Mills and his network of corrupt officials as much as officer Lake and his squad. They were in the motion of trying to influence the judges and officials in the southern states to get on the bandwagon. Officer Lake was trying to arrange it so that the judicial system would still be functioning without dismissing too many judges once the Shadowbox Operation was complete.

"So what are the next plans for me to attract the corrupt cops' attention, and persuade them to do as they have been doing many unfortunate youth in this part of the country by falsely arresting and charging them with crimes they didn't commit. Some even have been sent to prison for very lengthy sentences," Mark said with a bit of frustration and hitting his fist against the table.

"We need you to stay frequenting the streets where drugs are being sold, only don't sell anything or hold any drugs for anyone," Lake replied. "They may make a move at anytime, but we want to make sure you are innocent when they do. We will keep money in your pocket for your expenses and to portray the image of a successful drug dealer to make the local cops envy you when they see you dressing fancy and driving nice cars. Also, make it your business to visit the bars and clubs to hype your image. You may want to start by going to the club where Simona performs."

As officer Lake said the name Simona Mark's eyes lit up like a lantern. "Oh yeah, why didn't you tell me anything about Simona, and when will I meet more operatives from the FAOA to help me deal with the problems created by the fallen angels? Mark asked.

"Simona was going to be a surprise, but we will send you ops from the FAOA occasionally to let you know that you are not alone," Lake assured Mark while sipping his coffee and looking out the window.

There were roughly a hundred operatives from the FAOA in the Gulf Coast area. Many were busy trying to keep surveillance of the fallen angels and to make sure they didn't have plans to create some type of terroristic catastrophe with their mischievous ability to control the stardust. They were known to cause everything from fights between politicians to mass shootings at public events. The funny thing was that when the incident is over with the people committing the acts don't know why they did it, but the police have no choice but to take them to jail. The biggest victims of the sabotage were people in the poorest communities.

~

Attorney General Mills was determined to keep running his secret empire under President Harding's nose. He was a veteran and a lifelong bureaucrat in the ranks of the federal government. He had contacts throughout every intelligence agency, and was the secret ruler of a dangerous program began by the federal government.

As Mills entered the oval office, he thought to himself that he may run for president when President Harding's term was up in two years, and then he could take the fallen angels to their ultimate destination to shape the country as a select few sought fit. The only thing was his vision was nothing more than to treat the citizens of America like slaves by controlling and influencing their thoughts and actions. Only those at the top echelons of society would remain in control of their own actions by using their resources to make sure no one used stardust to control them, and by making sure anyone who tried would be severely punished.

"I want to congratulate on the effective use of the fallen angel program in various parts of our country, especially in the South," President Harding naively said praising Mills. Little did he know, the stardust was being used to create more junkies and drug dealers than gangster rap could ever been blamed for causing. President Harding assumed the fallen angels were being used to help alleviate the craving for street drugs, and to set up hardened criminals who have evaded the system of justice.

"Yes sir, Mr. President. We have been quite determined to rid the cities of America from their criminal behavior," Attorney General Mills responded with a fake smile. He knew his intentions with the fallen angels were to control the general population. He gave a damn how many were on drugs or selling drugs. He didn't even give a damn about how many people were being killed for no reason.

Attorney General Mills took a seat at the desk directly in front of the President. The President was looking through some files as Mills was hoping to himself that nothing in there suggested the real progress of the fallen angel program.

"So how are all the heads of all the fallen angel families doing with handing out the funds from the Better America program," President Harding asked Mills.

"They're doing a great job Mr. President," Mills Stated. "The Corleones from Alabama are distributing the funds to various families across the Gulf Coast and are getting rid of crime and encouraging a wholesome environment in the cities," he added while leaning toward the oval office desk and trying to look as sincere as he possibly could. "But we need more funds to keep things going smoothly."

Attorney General Mills was especially interested in the Gulf Coast Division. It was where he had the most loyal contacts and families who knew what was going on, but still continued to take the money and perform the most devious tasks. And, in the process, was almost ruining a whole culture of youth.

The money was spread across the South by the Corleones in Alabama. The family was of English and Italian ancestry, and had long roots in Mobile. They also had been with the fallen angels since the beginning of the group and the discovery of the stardust. They were just one of many families across the country given money by the federal government to keep the fallen angels controlling many of the things that happened in the communities of America. To receive the money, a family must already have extensive wealth and a prominent reputation among the area's elite.

"How much money do you need for your program Attorney General," the President asked. He was jotting down notes as they talked.

"The Corleones from Alabama are requesting one hundred million dollars for their loyal fallen angels who have kept the program successful. They need the money to keep their lifestyle status up to par with the requirements of the fallen angel program desires."

Attorney General Mills and the leaders of the fallen angels across the United States agreed that the families were to keep their households as tidy and bright as possible. The paint on their houses and cars had to be perfect and there must not be anything annoying to the eye in the vicinity. This vision of perfection carried on to include the members of the family to keep tidy with neat haircuts and perfect clothes at all times. According to their philosophy, this allowed them to judge others as being inferior to the standards of their society.

On the flip side, the leaders of the fallen angels did not put any trust in any member that did not partake in sinful activity such as adultery, murder, lying, and so forth. Those people who partook in such activity were their real brothers and sisters, like Adam and Eve, who sinned in the Bible. The fallen angels recognized god, but once a member have proven that they could be trusted, they revealed their true king, satan.

President Harding arose out of his seat and extended his arm to shake the hand of Attorney General Mills, and insured him that he would have the one hundred million dollars sent to the bank of his choice from the discretionary fund of Better America.

Chapter 14

Mark's little cousin, Joshua, held Mark's hand tight as they walked down the sidewalk leading up to Hurley elementary school. Taking his cousin to school was one of his duties that he agreed to do while he stayed at his mom's waiting to get back to the operation. Mark wanted to drop Joshua off, and leave rapidly before he saw any signs of Sarah. He knew it was a good chance that he would run in to her, because she had a few nieces and nephews that she took to Hurley Elementary occasionally. He still had feelings for Sarah, but now he was beginning to fall for Simona. He knew that their paths were meeting for a reason.

There were kids doing a variety of things as they waited for the bell to ring. Mark was watching his surroundings to see if anything unusual was taking place as he walked Joshua as close to his fifth grade class as possible. As he made it to the designated area where Joshua usually waited until the bell ringed for class, Joshua requested that he wait with him until the sound of the bell, which was in about seven minutes. He told Mark that there had been a series of fights in the past couple of days while the students waited to go to class. He felt safer with a grown up being by his side. Joshua was a relatively skinny kid and was a little on the soft side.

As they waited, two kids who appeared to be third or fourth graders lined up face to face with a crowd of kids surrounding them chanting them to begin fighting. It appeared to be the usual style showdown between kids from time to time. However, Mark noticed a slightly older looking kid step up and blow into one of the boys face as if he was infusing him with the stardust. He wondered had this stuff made it to the schools and playgrounds. That would be even more reason to stay in the operation.

It wasn't long before Mark's question was answered. With the older kid sitting back meditating and controlling the kid like a puppet, the kid who was blown the stardust had attacked the other kid with amazing strength for his age. It was clearly the adrenaline of the older kid controlling him with the stardust.

The controlled kid grabbed the other kid by the shirt and lifted him about a foot into the air, and then through him down with much force and began pounding on him like the LAPD done to Rodney King.

Mark stepped in immediately to stop the fight. He grabbed the raging kid, and immediately inhaled the stardust from his system. The other kid jumped up from the ground and dusted himself off with a slight tear rolling down his cheek. The older kid who initiated the incident walked away before Mark could even look towards his direction. Joshua watched from the sidelines, and was a little relieved that it wasn't him that was getting roughed up this morning.

Mark didn't waste time trying to give the kids a lecture. He knew that the kid using the stardust was probably the kid of some fallen angel member. He also knew that teaching your kid about this stuff was just like teaching them how to use a lethal weapon. This stuff had to be contained somehow Mark thought. It was a lot more dangerous than drugs in his opinion and becoming as ubiquitous.

Mark told his little cousin to be safe, and he released him by the front door to the hallway that his class was located on. He turned to walk back and started thinking that he hadn't seen the last of the usage of the stardust nor corrupt policemen encouraged to bend the law by the influence Attorney General Mills.

Before he could make it to the car, he heard a familiar voice calling his name aloud. It was, Sarah, his ex-girlfriend calling him as if she still commanded his attention like when they were in their controlling relationship. She still looked astounding Mark thought for a second, but he could never go back to someone who treated him in such a negative manner. She betrayed his trust and cheated on him with another man, even before she thought he was going through rough times.

"So, how has it been going?"Sarah asked like she was really interested in his recent life events. Mark still had a few barely visible bruises, but Sarah pretended not to see them.

"I've been doing fine," Mark responded. "I'm staying at my mother's for a while until I can get myself organized and find a job. How's everything at the firm. Is Mr. Cunningham still winning those court cases?" Mark inquired as Sarah looked toward the ground at the sound of Mr. Cunningham's name coming from Mark.

Mark didn't think it was necessary to let Sarah know anything about him actually performing a very important job since he left Virginia Central Law School. There was no need to sooth her curiosity about things since he knew he would never be with her again.

"It has been going very well at the firm," Sarah remarked. "There are the usual drug cases, the accident insurance cases, and divorces, but we recently were hired to represent a lawyer for attacking a man on the street with a knife after they bumped into each other. There was a big crowd watching the whole incident. The lawyer practiced civil rights, and was known around town to fight for the common people."

"Really, is it a murder case"? Mark asked starting to sense that it was the result of the fallen angels.

"No, it is a first degree felony assault though," She responded. "It's a very high profile case. He will likely be disbarred, but maybe we can get him off on a temporary insanity plea." Mark thought for a second, and realized that almost every suspect that committed a crime because of the mind control influence of the fallen angels deserved to at least get an insanity plea in court.

Mark decided to play the neutral role in responding about the case. He didn't want to appear too concerned. "Well, I hope justice is served in the case," he responded sounding like the neutral general that he was destined to be after the mission was completed.

"Nice seeing you though Sarah," Mark stated in an attempt to keep the conversation short. Most of the bruises were healed and he was ready to get back to the streets so that he could advance to stage two of the mission, getting fraudulently arrested and incarcerated by the corrupt system in Alabama.

Chapter 15

Remembering the advice of officer Lake and Goldy, Mark chose to not to partake in any illegal activity such as possessing and dealing drugs, but he was back hanging in the atmosphere. He was going to chill with Harold for a while. He would go the places he went, but would not do the street things he done. When he went on a legit job, he would work with him to make some extra money. He really didn't need it though, because the funds from the Falling Angels of America account would provide him with all the funds necessary to get by and plus extra money to help him look like he was balling.

Harold was a little paranoid from the incident with the police when Mark was assaulted by the two officers so he decided that it may be in his best interest to make money while riding in his Cadillac. They would stop by different hangout spots while waiting on drug buyers to contact his cellular phone. He only sold to the bottom line drug users that he was familiar with. He still made a decent living, though, with the money he received from working legitimate jobs.

They pulled up to one particular house that was built similar to the old shotgun houses that used to line the streets in the inner city of Mobile. A lady appeared at the door with a scarf on her head and some worn house shoes. There were about two or three kids standing beside her and peeking through the door while Harold entered. Mark sat patiently in the car watching traffic. He suspected that he would see a police before Harold came back to the car. What he didn't know was whether they would be policemen sent by Officer Lake to watch him or some of the corrupt officers affiliated with the fallen angels.

After Mark had waited about five or ten minutes, an odd looking man walked up to the passenger side car window where Mark was sitting. He wore old clothes that didn't really seem to go together, and they were coated with stains of dirt. His beard was several inches thick. He motioned for Mark to roll the window down further. Mark hesitated, because he sensed that the guy wanted to buy drugs or ask for money. Before Mark could discourage the man by telling him that he had neither drugs nor money to give him, the guy introduced himself.

"Hello, I'm Amos," the man said sounding a little more polished than his appearance spoke. Mark waited for him to get to his real motive of solicitations or ask him his name.

After a few seconds of anticipating further jabber, Mark told him his name. "My name is Mark." Given his involvement with a very unusual occupation of a strictly secretive operative, Mark assumed that it was the best thing to do. He didn't know who this guy was, and he didn't want to give him the indication that he was hiding anything.

"Oh, I know who you are young man," the guy spoke. The man was at least twenty years older than Mark. "Officer Lake sent me to meet you. I was dropped off by an associate at the corner up the street. I'm with the falling angels of America. I have been working for officer Lake since he began the organization to watch those devils, the fallen angels.

"There are plenty of us out here keeping an eye on the cities of America. You seem to be very important to Lake for not having been out here long. Maybe you will rise in the ranks fast."

Mark wasn't sure if Amos knew about the shadowbox operation or not. He wasn't sure how many of the agents from FAOA knew about it. So far he knew that Officers Lake, Goldy, and Paseney were fully aware of the operation and maybe a few people that were present at the Virginia Central Law School conference where he first opted to be a part of it, although he had yet to run into any of the other students.

"I sure hope I do, because I am very dedicated to the cause," Mark responded trying not to reveal any information to the odd guy without first hearing from Officer Lake.

"You will have us fellow ops around from now on. We don't want anything else like that police brutality stuff to occur anymore. Most of us keep more low profile duties that are usually safer," Amos said. "I know that you are setting up to enter the county jail to do some undercover stuff for the FAOA. That's about all I know, but it seems to be something much bigger."

Amos turned as he heard the door from the house that Harold went in open with the sound of two people chatting. "I will see you around comrade," Amos spoke then walked off like the common hobo he was disguised as.

Harold walked down the inclined yard to the car where Mark was waiting and trying to gather his thoughts about what just happened. He was ready to get his fancy vehicle and ride around completely legal to see if the cops really targeted young African Americans who appeared to have money. He knew that it shouldn't matter if the vehicle made the young black man fit the profile of a drug dealer. An individual citizen is free to ride in any vehicle they see fit, but not in the South, especially in Alabama.

Harold got in the car looking a little more uplifted. "First sale of the day buddy." It was a nice sixty dollars, " he said like he thought Mark would be happy for him. In a way, Mark was glad that his friend was lining his pockets with money. He sort of understood the drug game philosophy from the short time that he was acting as a dealer. A drug dealer wasn't giving crack smokers something they didn't want. It was like a business, and the goal was to make a profit. But, he knew that it wasn't a future in it, and the police often harassed you as long as they thought you were "dirty". And, if a man wasn't dirty,

they often made up charges on them anyway. That last
activity done by "dirty" cops, was a primary target of Lake
and the FAOA. The other targets were the fallen angels
and their stardust.

"Let's go by Martin's for a while and see if he has
any of those fine women over there," Harold said. Harold
wasn't faithful to his girlfriend, but he helped take care of
his family.

"Yea, that's cool. I haven't seen him since I was in
the hospital," Mark responded. The talk about women
caused Mark to think of Sarah and Simona. He had loved
Sarah, and had been faithful for the most part. He
wondered should he put all trust in Simona just because
she was affiliated with his lifetime commitment, the Falling
Angels of America. The one thing he knew was that he
wanted to be with her as soon as he got the chance.

~

When Mark and Harold walked into Martin's
apartment he was at the computer studying profiles of
single women on the most popular dating site in the city.
Mark stood over his shoulder to get a peek at what the site
had to offer, although he wasn't looking for anyone

himself. He was just curious. He never experimented with online dating sites, but he had heard many interesting stories about it.

"Woa, that girl is awesome," Harold said. "She is pretty, got body, and she's independent," he said excitedly with his hand rubbing his chin.

"Yes, she is," Martin added. "I've met over ten women on these dating sites. I went to bed with most of them." Martin wasn't the type to brag about his escapades, but he wanted his friends to know that he was successful at what he was doing although he had yet to find one that was willing to settle down with him.

"So what have you guys been up to?" Martin asked as he was closing the site out getting ready to shut the shut the computer down.

"Nothin much," Mark replied. "Don't shut it down yet. I need to search for some luxury cars on craigslist."

"Luxury cars?" Martin asked.

"Yes, I need it for my secret ops job. The directors want me to purchase a fancy car along with some expensive clothes and jewelry as part of my undercover duties. I was thinking of a Mercedes or a Jaguar."

Martin typed in Craiglist.com in the web address search bar while looking a little concerned about the whole Falling Angels of America ordeal. The site appeared on the screen of the computer, and Martin continued by typing in 2030 Mercedes in the search bar. A list of new Mercedes sedans was listed in a vertical row. Most of the vehicles were black, but a few were white or red.

"What's the price on the red 500 series at the bottom of the page?" Mark asked

Martin clicked on the picture to bring up the information related to the car. "Seventy-one thousand with only twenty thousand miles on it," Martin said.

"That's the one for me," Mark responded. It was the hottest looking car on the site. It was fire red with twenty inch chrome rims. It also had a sunroof. Mark knew that it would attract the attention of the crooked cops. The cops that were either out to harass and frame young fly brothers and the cops that were simply out to illegally confiscate money and possessions would be highly tempted. It would be impossible for them to know how he obtained the nice car and things, because he was associated with Harold, who had a blemished criminal record. The way the FAOA looked at it, it wasn't a crime to hang with individuals that made some serious mistakes in the past.

"Well, go ahead and print it out Martin," Harold stated. "I have to get back to hustling. Plus I've got two missed calls that I need to return. One's my old lady and the other is some serious doe."

Mark grabbed the printout and followed Harold out the door and down the stairs to Harold's car. The two rode off while Mark called the contact number on the car printout. He thought that he might enjoy riding the nice car while it lasted. The good thing about it is that it would be his when the operation was complete. The car would be his along with many other luxuries, but what he really anticipated was the opportunity to govern over a mostly free and independent America.

Chapter 16

Simona sat in the 500 Mercedes Benz with her seat inclined midways back and her hand resting on Mark's thigh, while he was in the driver's seat sipping on a light draft beer. They were parked in the parking lot of a normally busy shopping center, but there weren't many cars in the lot, because the center was getting ready to close in about fifteen minutes. Simona's friend and bodyguard, James, stood at the rear of the car smoking a cigarette. Lake felt as if she was important to the operation and deserved to have some protection so he assigned her a bodyguard whom she had grown to develop a friendship with.

"You know what Mark I brought some stardust for you to practice with," Simona said in a soft tone." You have been in the FAOA for long enough now to be an expert at the mind control game."

"I don't really like the stuff much though," Mark answered. "It takes a person's ability to choose freely his decisions," he added.

"Remember, we only use it for defense or to make good things happen," she said. "We don't do tons of wrong and say that the result is going to be for the better like the fallen angels do. They do things like wreck a bus, and say that it is going to make people walk more, which will lead to a cleaner atmosphere. I mean, really, they once used stardust to make a guy cheat big time on his taxes, and said it paved the way for tax reform. The guy got like fifteen years, and he had paid his taxes on time every year before that. He never knew what came over him."

Simona pulled out a designer scarf that appeared to be a very nice and clean piece of garment, and handed it to Mark. "Put it up to your nose and act like your smelling it," Simona said.

"It smells like CHANEL perfume," Mark uttered. He knew that it was filled with stardust, but he couldn't tell whether or not it was in his system. He wasn't sure how much it took to actually be effective on someone.

"Now, get out the car and stand by James. Ask him a question or something, and then when he looks away exhale for a little while. Think about James handing you a cigarette without giving any indication that you want one, and he will hand it to you without even asking."

Mark got out the car and stood by James like he just interested in casual conservation. He asked him how long had he been licensed to carry a gun, and then he exhaled slowly. Immediately after exhaling, he got quiet and imagined that James was handing him a cigarette. Five seconds hadn't past before James pulled out a cigarette and offered it to Mark. Mark told him thanks, and then opened the car door to get back in to tell Simona the outcome of her little assignment.

"This stuff is brilliant," Mark exclaimed. "He handed me the cigarette as soon as I meditated on him giving it to me just like you said. Why don't we have anyone in North Korea and Russia to brain wash those leaders over there to hand over their nuclear weapons?"

"Maybe we will one day, but they have specialists over there in their government who work with stardust also," Simona replied." "The government officials have guards that secretly keep the stuff from around them. Anyways, we are focused on keeping our government from using the stuff on its own citizens. We have to get Attorney General Mills out of office as soon as possible."

"So exactly how is he connected to the South and Mobile, Alabama specifically?" Mark asked. "I mean, he is based in Washington D.C."

"He pays the leaders of the cells of fallen angels all across the country, but he shows particular interests in the Mobile area," Simona explained. He calls them families, and as you know, they tend to have a Nazi mentality. Some of the families would exterminate entire sections of the population if allowed to do so. There's been talk in the Justice Department to build many more prisons in Alabama in which they would use the stardust to influence people, who they deem unfit for society, to do criminal acts, and place them in the prisons."

"So if we get him out and stop the funding of the families we can keep anymore unnecessary crime from occurring, and save many unsuspecting people their freedom," Mark replied.

"Partially correct," Simona said while folding up the scarf. "We also have to seize the stardust from the government and as much as we can from the families. All that we can't get will eventually expire. This stuff is only usable for about a week. They can't create any, unless they get it from the government. Attorney General Mills was sure to keep the process top secret."

"And how will infiltrating the cops in the South lead us to AG Mills?" Mark asked.

"Most of them work for the local families of the fallen angels who are under the command of Mills. The leaders of the families get millions of dollars from Mills every year. The cops only get a portion of that money.

Once we get them entangled in a major scheme to falsely imprison law abiding citizens, we will use that as evidence to overthrow the current administration."

"Sounds extremely difficult," Mark replied.

"We also will use a show of force if necessary. We don't expect the fallen angels to give up without a fight. Not all of the cops are in with the fallen angels. In fact the majority of them are trying to do the right thing about the law, and some don't even know that the stardust exists. We will use those officers, and the agents that Lake have on his side to secure our newly gained positions of authority. You have been carefully selected to be in the top position of the new government." Simona spoke as if she was very confident that the operation known as shadowbox would be a success, and that he was the person for the job and for her.

"One more thing before we go," Simona stated trying not to keep James waiting outside of the car for too long. She pulled the scarf back out and raised it to her nose to inhale the stardust from it. She blew into Mark's nostrils for what seemed to be a full minute. He immediately felt a warm sensation through his body. Then, she began to kiss him on the mouth while rubbing his body up and down as if they were going to make out right there in the car.

"It feels like I'm getting a double pleasure," Mark whispered. "Am I getting your sensations along with my own sensational feelings?"

"Yes, it's one of the coolest things about this stuff," Simona whispered back with her eyes squinted like a cat and her lips curved into a sneaky smile.

They cuddled for a few minutes then she let James know they were ready to go. James didn't know as much about the activities of the FAOA, but his loyalty to Simona was undisputed. The three rode away from the parking lot with Mark and Simona anticipating more future escapades. For now, she would go to the club where she performed and Mark would go to his luxury Mercedes.

Chapter 17

The meeting place that Attorney General Mills
agreed to meet Mr. Corleone was an old public school
building that appeared to be abandoned from the
appearance of it, although the lawn was maintained to
prevent it from becoming a public nuisance. Inside there
were several halls of empty classrooms, but in one of the
larger classrooms on the shortest hall there was a long oak
meeting table with oak chairs lined along it. This is where
the leaders of the local fallen angels met with AG Mills or
other members of the Justice Department's secret branch.
Today, Mr. Corleone had two of his most trusted fallen
angel soldiers from Southern Alabama, and AG Mills had
his trusted assistant who was also a fallen angel.

"The number of hoodlums and thugs incarcerated in the local jails and prisons have been decreasing lately Mr. Corleone. What's the problem," Mills asked angrily in a raised voice. He considered thugs and hoodlums to be anyone without a fancy job and down on their luck at the time. He didn't care if they planned to elevate their position in the future, and they really didn't even have to commit a crime. Walking around town enough at certain times because a person didn't own a vehicle was enough for Mills to want the person locked up. To help accomplish this, he wanted Mr. Corleone to see if the fallen angels could influence them to fall into some type of criminal trap.

"Several judges in the district court have a tendency to reduce the sentences of many criminals and dismiss cases for various reasons like improper procedure on behalf of the police and lack of evidence," Corleone replied. "They're not seeing it our way Mr. Mills."

"We have to get more judges on the pay roll or get someone close to them to obfuscate their thinking with the stardust," Mills stated. "We need to make them see the defendants as they are, menaces to our society and the new order of the United States that we are trying to develop." Mills spoke as if he was Fidel Castro when he sought to imprison or get rid of certain sectors of the Cuban population in the early eighties.

Mr. Corleone arose from his seat, and walked over by the window where he formed a space between the blinds with his fingers to get a view of the parking lot. Mr. Corleone was an older guy in his late fifties, but he wasn't so old to the point where he couldn't grasp the revolutionary power that the fallen angels possessed with the use of their stardust. He was one of the first family leaders to make a deal with Attorney General Mills. He also had possessed a small fortune prior to receiving money from the fallen angels society, but not nearly as much as he had gained since.

"Did you sweep the building for possible bugs Mr. Mills?" Corleone asked AG Mills as he closed the gap in the blinds.

"Of course Mr. Corleone," Mills replied. "I had my guys from the local office check the place twice, and no one would be listening to us anyway. We have the entire city cooperating with our program or on our payroll. We just have to get more of those judges to lose their religion a little bit in exchange for a ubiquitous dominion." Mills or Corleone had no idea that people in their organizations were working with Lake under the counteractive umbrella of the Falling Angels of America. The organization's name was even similar to Mill's fallen angels as to confuse anyone who became aware of their heroic efforts.

Mills gained the influence of many politicians and law enforcement officers by promising that they would eventually be helping their causes by breaking the rules,

152

but others were simply in it for financial gain or they were just naturally evil. Whatever the case, the fallen angels were slowly gaining control of the country's most vital systems that assured America to be the land of the free.

"I don't want to take the chance that someone like a self righteous judge will expose our alliances in the city, so I will see if I can get some of my fallen angels to use their skills to make some of the judges change their mind about releasing these misfits into the streets," Mr. Corleone stated. They will do it with the stardust, and without the knowledge that they are being controlled."

"We will need more funds to arrange this latest effort to cleanse our streets though," Corleone said.

"I will arrange for an extra three million dollars to be added to your account this month," Mills replied. It shouldn't take much more than that to get the job done."

"We can actually use a lot more, but that will do for now," Corleone said. "Our fallen angels need money to stay motivated, and they could use some programs to illustrate what the whole fallen angel image is all about. We need our own celebrities that are full of the glamorous light of the original fallen angel, Lucifer."

Mills and the leaders of the fallen angels in Washington D.C. had always toyed with the destiny of celebrities, but they had yet to produce a celebrity in Alabama. They knew that celebrities contained the power to influence the general population with their fame. If the celebrities agreed to include the fallen angel propaganda in their entertainment, they contributed to their success by buying them radio play and paying for expensive videos to promote their album.

"We know of this one young lady who has been playing the local scene, and we would like to bring her into the plan and make her an idol for the members in Alabama and the Gulf Coast," Mr. Corleone said with the look of enthusiasm. "Her name is Simona, and she seems to be the perfect match for our society."

"I can only provide my support for her if she is capable of being a national or maybe international star that will demonstrate to the entire organization the true image of perfection," Mills stated. "But, if it will make the families in the South happy to have her come from their region, so be it."

The true image of perfection that Mills was referring to was an image of a person without any flaws in their appearance or character, but whose loyalty was to the philosophy of the fallen angels that they possessed supreme knowledge of god himself. However, they could use any type of deceit or other evil tactics to obtain their desires. These tactics were often illegal according to the laws of the United States, and even included the use of severe oppression or slavery.

"She is most certainly capable of making our cause advance greatly," Corleone stated with his hand resting on the shoulder of AG Mills. She sings like a real angel and has the sex appeal to entice the guys and make the young ladies wish they were her." What they didn't know was that she was deeply dedicated to the FAOA, and a sworn enemy to their fallen angels' agenda.

~

One week later

Mark was quietly turning the key to the doorknob on his apartment door when he heard the voice of what sounded to be a policeman saying "I need you to come with me sir." He turned around to see a guy only a few years older than himself. He was wearing a conservative suit, and had a holster with a nine millimeter tucked into it. He immediately thought that this was the big score, some corrupt law enforcement official had taken enough of seeing him riding around in the Benz and had decided to take him down without cause just like Officer Lake predicted. Mark was preparing to surrender like the protocol that he and Officer Lake and Goldy had practiced. He turned towards the door with his hands in the air and his legs spread apart. Then, to Mark's surprise, the guy told him to put his hands down and that he was taking him to meet the FAOA lead team. Officer Lake had arranged for someone to secretly transport him to a meeting that Mark hadn't been aware of.

They slowly drove down the street without saying much. Since the agent wasn't talking, Mark assumed it was best if he didn't ask any questions. Officer Lake and the other members of the operation would explain everything to him when he arrived to the secret meeting place. The windows on the car were darkly tinted like the cars driven often by government officers. He was beginning to feel like he was already transitioning to the Neutral General position, but he was hoping that he didn't have to spend time in jail to get there. However, he knew that he wouldn't give up. It was the only way he and Simona would fulfill their destiny.

The agent pulled up to a huge house that was a little smaller than a mansion on the gulf front of the Gulf of Mexico. He entered a garage that went below the level of the house that was some type of secret entrance to the basement. Once they exited the car and went inside there was a door that required a code to open it up, they went inside where there were absolutely no windows. The place had a very comfortable feel, but there were electronic devices scattered around the room which made it feel like a surveillance facility instead of a getaway home. Mark noticed a door in the back of the place with a glittering smoke coming from underneath. It looked like stardust, but he had never seen that much at one time. In the center of the room sat Officers Lake, Goldy, and Paseney at a large dinner table.

"Come have a seat with us Mark," Paseney stated. She had her hair in a conservative ponytail and was wearing her normal attire of dark business suits.

"The reason we called you here today was because of some important and alarming news we received from our inside connections in D.C.," Paseney said like she was concerned and gladdened at the same time.

Mark was anticipating the new information, but the room grew silent for a minute with the leaders of the FAOA staring at each other and him also as to figure which one was going to reveal the news. Finally, Officer Paseney decided to continue.

"The fallen angels have chosen to make Simona their prize possession for their efforts in the Gulf Coast region. They decided that she was of the material that the fallen angels could grow their campaign with a little nurturing in their philosophical ideas and enticement with superiority ideals. She contacted us as soon as Mr. Corleone left the club after promising her that she would become a superstar if she worked with them."

"Is she going to leave her duties in the FAOA?" Mark asked.

"Of course not," said Goldy. "It presents the perfect chance for us to have someone loyal to us inside the fallen angels with access to the top leaders, especially in the Southern branch. Officer Lake briefs with AG Mills from time to time, but he will not provide him with much information on the fallen angels. He does acknowledge that they do still exist though. We have to depend on informants for the Falling angels of America to report what their next move is going to be. There still isn't any indication that he knows that our organization exists."

"Once you are taken in by the corrupt local officers working with the fallen angels, communications with Simona will become an extremely difficult task, because we will begin the transaction to take over the federal government including the local governments in Southern Alabama," Officer Lake explained to Mark. Mark's eyes were starting to wander over to the room with the sparkling smoke oozing out of the bottom.

" Officer Lake, Goldy, and myself don't want anything to happen to either one of you. You will have bodyguards in the jail, but we want Simona to stay undercover in AG Mills organization as long as possible or until the mission is complete," Officer Paseney said. "She will keep us abreast of the situation within the organization while we seek to get AG Mills and as many fallen angels as possible locked up, and while we try to get you released to a safe location.

"There are a few more things Mark before we return you to your apartment though," Officer Lake said. "We want you to wear dark clothes, but still keep them flashy. It is preferable that you wear mostly black."

"Why should I wear black clothing," Mark asked. "It seems kind of creepy to me."

"The fallen angels and the cops that work for them hate to see people wear black," Lake replied. "They are obsessed with the color white. It represents the light of their fallen angel originator, Lucifer. In their teachings, anything black is seen as being in opposition to his rule."

"Yea, I have heard something like that from a friend in college," Mark said. "He was trying to convince me that Lucifer was the real father of lights. Maybe he was a part of the fallen angels."

"More than likely his a member of the group or had been influenced by them," Lake replied while trying to switch the topic of discussion.

Officer Lake stood up and told Mark to come with him as he walked to the room with the stardust contained in it. He grabbed a box that resembled a beer cooler and opened it to reveal to Mark the contents. One hundred percent pure stardust was contained in the box. The material was transported there from a secret lab in Virginia.

"We are going to send this box of stardust along with you for you to use if needed," Officer Lake stated. "All you have to do is leave a rag or a piece of cloth material in there for about five minutes, and take the rag with you when you're out in the town. As you know, you can control unsuspecting individuals' thoughts and actions with it. It will help if the cops try to beat you up again."

After Mark received the box, Lake's assistant officer led him to the car to take him back to the apartment.

Chapter 18

It was getting close to sunset as Mark decided to ride the Benz to the corner store, which was also a hangout, to meet Harold. It was the same block that Mark was assaulted by the police on, and it was his first time returning to the spot. This time he was driving a Benz and wearing black jeans with a black t-shirt, but no skullcap or bandana, which could easily be confused with gang attire. Either way his chances were increased to get fraudulently arrested or beaten again, but this time he had the stardust to prevent a bad assault. Also, if they chose to assault him again, Lake had promised that the operation would go to the next level at that point. It would be enough for him to push for a transition. Especially, with agents from the Falling Angels of America not far away with surveillance equipment posted on the block.

Mark pulled into a parking lot near the rear of the store. He got out the car and locked the doors to the Benz, although he was safe in this part of town. The local people knew his face now from hanging with Harold. They also knew that the cops had beaten him up so they knew he couldn't be a cop or an informant. There were also some people from the FAOA that Lake sent in the vicinity, although Mark couldn't tell who they were.

Mark entered the store and asked the store clerk for Harold. He pointed upstairs where there were a couple of pool tables and a stereo for the local hustlers. Not just anyone was allowed to go to the "top floor" as it was called. The store owner had to know you or you had to be with someone he knew. There was a little bit of everything going on up there like drug dealing and gambling.

"What's up homie," Mark said has he greeted Harold with a handshake.

There were two other guys playing pool in the room with Harold. Harold was text messaging with his girlfriend as he took swigs from a bottle of beer. Mark sat in a chair next to where Harold was sitting.

"Hey, you mind if I get one of those cold beers," Mark asked Harold. "And, after you get through making love on that phone I want to see you on that pool table."

"Oh, grab one buddy," Harold responded. "I been waiting to see if you still got your pool skills anyway," he added. Mark was a bit of a gambler since high school. It was the only thing that he really had street about him. He also was a pretty good pool player, and would often win extra money in school playing his college friends.

Harold grabbed a pool stick for the both of them while Mark turned on the light above the pool table. "What will be the wager for the winner of the game," Harold asked with a sly smile on his face.

"How about a good fifty dollars," Mark quickly answered. "It will make it worth your time." Fifty dollars wasn't much for Mark now that he had funds coming in from the FAOA. It also wasn't much for Harold with all the money he received from hustling. Mark was a little worried that Harold may get caught in the mix of his dealing with the FAOA, but he knew he should be able to get him out if everything went as planned.

"Yea, we can play for a cool Grant," Harold replied. "Rack em up partner. I might just run the table on you."

Mark racked the balls in the usual form for a game of eight-ball. Harold in return broke the balls up with much strength then took a long sip of his beer.

"I see you wearing all black today like a real gangsta. What does that represent," Harold inquired. Harold had figured that it was something to the way Mark was dressed, because Mark usually dressed in traditional casual gear like polo shirts and blue jean pants.

"It's something I got to do for my job," Mark answered not trying to reveal anything to the other guys that were in the room with them. "I'll tell you about it later."

Mark and Harold exchanged shots for about ten minutes while talking casual conversation. Mark glanced out the window located in the front of the pool room from time to time to see if he could see any cops pulling up or rolling by. He knew that the Benz parked outside would attract attention from any cops tempted to harass young males. The good thing about it is that the entire store, including the poolroom, was a legitimate privately owned establishment. If the police wanted to bust the place, they would need a legal search warrant signed by a judge. It was simply the law, although in this city it was often ignored, but if they tried it today, Officer Lake and the rest of the FAOA team would have proof that they totally ignored the laws of the constitution.

Finally, after the two guys shooting pool next to Harold and Mark left the room, Harold spoke up. "I forgot to tell you the last time we spoke, but one of my buddies was in Mr. Cunningham's law office the other day, and said he seen Sarah in there all cozy with Mr. Cunningham."

"I sort of knew that's who she must have been cheating on me with," Mark replied. "She was always working late, and she said his name while in conversation too much. Sometimes she even called him by his first name so I knew their relationship was a little deeper than an employee and boss situation. Anyhow, I have Simona by my side now, and I got a good hunch that she's going to be around for awhile.

"That's not the worst of it," Harold said eagerly wanting to reveal more details about the conversation. "He said that they were talking about some organization called the fallen angels. Isn't that the guys you said were enemies of your secret team and were doing all of that foul stuff in our community."

"Yes, if that's true she's in deep trouble," Mark said with deep concern. "Did he give any detail concerning what Mr. Cunningham's dealings were with the organization?"

"Not much," Harold replied. "It was something about him being paid a bunch of money to not do a good job representing particular clients that he was hired to defend."

"Those clients that he is misrepresenting are probably innocent of the crimes they are charged with," Mark stated. "That's how we're going to expose the crooked system in the end. They have the cops, district attorneys, and some judges trying to cleanse the city of all the people who they dislike simply because of their color or lifestyles.

Mark couldn't believe it. Mr. Cunningham's law office, including Sarah, was in bed with the fallen angels. He wasn't in love with Sarah any longer, but he sure didn't want her to ruin her life knowing what he knew about the affairs of the fallen angels. Now, Sarah and Simona were inside the fallen angels. Maybe the FAOA could convince Sarah and Mr. Cunningham to cooperate, and inform Officer Lake and the team on the activities of the fallen angels like Simona was doing. It may have to wait until the team was ready to make their final move to transitioning, but the sooner the better.

While Mark was contemplating on the information that he was being told Sarah, Harold was lining the cue up to make the eightball in the top right corner after Mark had scratched on the last shot. Harold concentrated for about five seconds before slamming the ball into the corner.

"That was an easy fifty dollars buddy," Harold spoke as if he was a professional billiard player.

"Awe, you got lucky that time friend," Mark replied. "I'll win the next time we play. We will make it a hundred dollars even."

Mark got Harold's pool stick from him and handed him a crisp fifty from a small wad of money. He went to put both of their pool sticks on the rack and glanced out the window to see two local cops slowly pass by. The first car was a marked car, but the second car was unmarked with tinted windows and a couple of antennas extending from it. He also saw a few guys hanging out across the street. One of the guys was wearing what appeared to be an earphone radio. The guy put his hand up making the sign of an L. He knew that stood for, Lake, his head officer from the Falling Angels of America. They were really looking out for him, like angels, so when the cops decided to make their move, there would be witnesses to any misdeeds, and there would be evidence to prove their wrongdoing.

Chapter 19

The room in Mark's apartment was dimly lit, but Mark sat fixated on a story in the local newspaper while Simona sat next to him eating a bowl of cheerios. The story was under the heading "Suspect Shoots Man for Fifty Dollar Sneakers." This was just one of the many bazaar stories being talked about across town in the last week. The most alarming was a small war among two rival gangs who were at a truce with each other for the past fifteen years. It was unclear what they were conflicting about, but Mark sensed that the fallen angels were involved with this situation and the further increase in crime lately. These types of things occurred without the influence of stardust sometimes, but lately there were many crimes committed by individuals and groups that didn't have the capacity to do them unless they were involuntarily controlled to do such things. The gangs that had begun to war weren't into violence anymore, and had cooperated with each other in the drug game for years now.

"This is truly a shame," Mark uttered as he almost slammed the newspaper down on the table. "The gang violence has the fallen angel influence all over it. And, each time an incident occurs, there are two or more people eliminated or hurt. The ones who commit the crime and the ones who are victimized by the violence are taken from the community. I would say that it was a part of their lifestyle, but Harold knows many of these kids, and he says that they aren't even capable of the type of violence on their own. Most of them just claim to be in a gang to be a part of something."

Simona sat listening quietly as Mark spoke angrily. "Well, I see young guys talking to the fallen angel people under Mr. Corleone sometime," she stated. "I think I saw one of the guys on the news like a few days later for robbing a convenience store. He was twenty-four years old, and his only record up to that point was for public intoxication."

"Really, it's becoming a common occurrence that these youth are committing an unheard of number of crimes lately," Mark replied. "I bet their filling their head with stardust, and then putting the idea to do multiple bad things on their mind. It's just a matter of time before they do some horrible act. All the police have to do is keep a tab on them, and they have the kid before the crime is even committed. Then, they get them to hire a fraudulent lawyer like Mr. Cunningham to represent them. The kids never have a chance."

Simona stood up and walked to the kitchen sink to rinse the bowl that she was eating from while Mark continued to rattle on about the current state of crimes in the area. Simona had been working undercover as a diva idol for Attorney General Mills and Mr. Corleone for several weeks now. The fallen angels hadn't revealed too many details about their devious activities or future plans yet, but she could sense that they were up to something catastrophic. Mr. Corleone mostly tried to convince her to dislike anything that appeared to be dark or had the essence of a spiritually minded figure. Everything she associated with had to be proud and overly concerned with worldly things. In his mind, he knew that was what would make Lucifer happy, but he had yet to unravel who is main audience to satisfy was.

She came back and sat in Mark's lap then removed the newspaper gently from his hands. "I want you at the club as much as possible from now on," Simona said as she begun to run her fingers over Mark's hair. "If you keep coming around with your present dress and style, I think the fallen angels will make a move possibly using some illegal arrest. I know Officers Lake and Goldy will be sure to have some loyal secret ops from our organization, the FAOA, to protect you if things get out of hand."

Mark reluctantly agreed, because he wasn't sure if he was ready to spend time away from Simona. He knew that he couldn't be seen getting to close to her if things were to get closer to its destination of him completing the mission. However, if the fallen angels thought that he was influencing their future star from becoming their dream fallen angel icon for the South, they would probably be more eager to see him in jail. The image that he was portraying for Lake and the Falling Angels of America was in strong contrast to the wicked image so adored by the fallen angels. Also, it was an image that was part of who he really was. He couldn't pass a homeless person on the street without giving him his spare change, while Attorney General Mill's fallen angel's mentality was to have the hobo put away for life it was possible.

Mark took another look at the newspaper and stood up while pulling Simona close to him. "Baby you know what. I am going to make my presence at the club from now on. Every day that you perform I will be there. I will get to see you and I will offer the dirty fallen angels and the dirty cops some bait to finally proceed with the mission. I've already heard from Lake and Gordy that my name is starting to ring bells since I have been sporting my Benz around town and dressing shady so it's getting close for them to make a move. They hardly let any young black guy that looks to be doing well last long without being under control of their fallen angel wings.

Sarah responded by holding him around the waist and assuring him that she would be there for him just like the mission was planned. Something that was once a prearranged union was now a destined fate.

~

New Orleans

Martin was very excited that Mark was going to try to get him involved with the operation. He was glad to be out of the service, but getting a chance to be involved with the likes of an intelligence job was his dream. The only catch was getting Officer Lake to go along with letting Martin cover for him when Mark went to the bar where Simona performed.

The club now secretly belonged to the fallen angels and Mr. Corleone, who also thought that they owned Simona. But, Simona was a devoted member of the Falling Angels of America, and had agreed to marry Mark upon completion of the mission whether she loved him or not. The good part about it was that Mark and Simona had fell into deep love.

Martin and Harold had played an unofficial role in the operation thus far by providing Mark with assistance from time to time with planning how to become the perfect bait for the local crooked cops. Now, Martin would become an official member or the FAOA if Lake agreed.

Harold was still to assist Mark unofficially at times and would cooperate with Mark at the bar also. He was still crucial in making the crooked cops feel that they could violate all of Mark's civil rights when they arrested him like they done many other innocent people in the city. They knew Harold was into street occupations although he was rather smart at it. He had yet to catch their attention.

On the other hand, Mark was now clean, but he was exemplifying success and didn't fit their profile for a person that should have the things that he did. He dressed in dark clothes and had the aura of a true Christian vagabond, which was something that the cops working for the fallen angels despised.

Mark and Martin were to meet Officer Lake in a secret hideout in an abandoned building that was set up for training recruits in the city of New Orleans where the fight against the fallen angels was also underway, but there wasn't a mission as important as Mobile's anywhere in the country. Mobile was where AG Mills had his most vested interests, because the fallen angels were trying to make the area their secret headquarters. The most loyal followers of the fallen angel's ideology were located there.

The two pulled up to the building, which looked like an old retail store. The building's windows were covered with faded tan paper and there was a parking lot in the rear of the store where Mark parked his red Benz.

The two got out of the door and walked to the door where they were met by a huge guy wearing a black turtleneck and black pants with black steel toe boots. He was a guard entrusted by Officers Lake and Goldy to keep anyone other than the ops from the FAOA from entering the facility. Mark said the secret code word, "NGTF", which stood for never going to fall. The guard opened the door for them to enter.

Officers Lake, Goldy, and Paseney were sitting at a table discussing matters related to the current situation of the Shadowbox operation. There were several other operatives and guards spread across the room. It was very similar to the setup in Baldwin County, but it didn't have a room for storing stardust.

"Officer Lake this is, Martin, my friend that I told you about when we spoke on the phone two days ago,"

Mark stated. "He's interested in joining the operation, and he has solid military credentials. I really need someone that I know and can trust now that this thing is about to get underway."

"How are you so sure that the locals will make their move on you soon?" Officer Paseney inquired.

"I spoke with Simona, and we agreed that I should come to the club flashing like I'm a big time young black male while Mr. Corleone and some of the other families of the fallen angels are watching," Mark responded. "To make it more tempting, I plan to make a move on Simona as if I'm just meeting her. She will respond like she's interested, which will hurt their pride to have their newly created idol being influenced by a character such as myself."

"Quite a plan Mark," Gordy stated. "This is exactly why we chose you to become the Neutral General. You show a knack for critical but judgmentally fair thinking.

"So what role do you believe Martin should play with these final tasks related to the shadowbox operation," Paseney asked. "We will already have several ops in place from the FAOA using stardust to make sure none of the fallen angels try to control the corrupt cops to badly assault or try to kill you."

"He will be directly with me if anything goes down," Mark responded. "My friend Harold will be there also as a witness, but I would like you to train Martin on the usage of the stardust to control situations. He is the only one that I trust. Those officers could have killed me when they put me in the hospital, and I wasn't flashing as I am now to tempt the local officers even more. They just randomly targeted me and assaulted me without cause."

"I will grant your request since you will soon be the boss anyhow," Lake said with a short laugh.

"Great, you won't regret it Officer Lake," Mark responded happily.

Mark had begun to demonstrate his ability to lead the country. Picking his friend Martin to bring into the operation was sign that he could designate responsibility among others. And, he could now go into dangerous territory without being insecure about whether he would make it out alive.

Chapter 20

It was about 4:00pm when Mark and Martin made it back to the city of Mobile, which was having a bit of bad weather on this Friday. The streets were covered with rain puddles from a bad rainstorm that occurred a little earlier that day, which was not out of the ordinary for the city. Mark drove the Mercedes carefully while navigating to meet Harold at his place. Mark wanted to update Harold on everything before they went to the club where Simona performed. He also wanted to introduce both Martin and Harold to the usage of the stardust. It would come in handy if they were skilled at using the powerful dust.

The two got out of the car and walked cautiously to the door while looking around for anything unusual. Harold answered the door after the second knock. He was anticipating their arrival since they had talked about their planned meeting if things went as planned in New Orleans. They were followed from New Orleans by a black ford sedan, but it wasn't anything to be alarmed about. It was most likely some comrades from the FAOA that Lake sent as extra protection and intelligence.

Mark and Martin entered the house eagerly after being welcomed in by Harold. Harold's black Labrador was present and wagging his tail at the arrival of new guest. It would be perfect to use for practice with the stardust. Harold was dressed in black club attire as well as Martin and Harold for extra offense to any fallen angels at the club tonight.

"So did your commanding officers agree to let us in on the operation," Harold asked.

"Yes, it's called the shadowbox operation, and the code word is shadowbox just in case you have to communicate with anyone from the Falling Angels of America," Mark replied.

The code word was kept secret among the ops in the FAOA. It was crucial for the operation, because many of the ops from the FAOA really didn't know each other. They were located and operated by the central command of Officers Lake, Goldy, and Paseney, but mostly Lake gave the orders for now. Goldy would take the leading charge once Mark entered the inner confines of the local county jail.

"This is the plan," Mark began. "We all will enter the club dressed as we are. Harold it would be good if you put your black shades on. That will suggest to them that the cops could get away with anything that they wish with concerns to our legal rights to attend the club and talk to whomever we liked. They would stereotype us in a minute with those dark shades."

Mark continued talking about the plans for the night. "We will order one beer each and sit at an open table so that the alcohol won't be an issue and we won't get confused with someone who is actually doing illegal stuff. We don't want to get it confused on whether or not the police actually find drugs at the table we're sitting at."

Martin and Harold listened intently although they weren't sure if it would result in the police falsely arresting them. They thought that it was very likely though given the statistics on people claiming to be falsely arrested in Mobile County the last couple of years. The ultimate pushing point would be when Mark intertwined with Mr. Corleone's and AG Mills new fallen angel idol of pride, Simona.

"After Simona takes a break from singing her first song, I will meet her at the bar and begin talking to her while flashing a wad of money to buy us drinks from the bar," Mark continued. "I will make sure Mr. Corleone sees my little interaction with Simona, whom he has no idea is really my girlfriend. They're sure to bite."

"And, what role will the stardust play in all this," Martin asked.

"It will play a big role," Mark replied. "We may even have to use it to get the security guard to let us in the club, but mostly to make sure things don't get out of hand when the cops try to arrest us. Anyway, we need to run a practice using the stardust real fast with both of you."

Mark pulled a blue dry facecloth from his pocket that contained a very concentrated amount of stardust within in it. He had obtained the stardust from Officer Lake while they met in New Orleans. The cloth almost had a glow to it if one stared at it too long. He handed the cloth to Martin and instructed him to inhale from it as if it was menthol cigarette, and then blow into the air vicinity of Harold's facial location. He then instructed him to think of Harold hitting him in the face with his fist.

Before he could react Harold had took a violent swing at his head, and just barely stopping before he landed one right on the left side of his cranium. With Harold even knowing that he was about to be controlled by Martin, he was just barely able to prevent from striking him. Had he not known, Martin probably would have been laying on the ground from the strength that Harold had in his arm. "Dam, I almost knocked you out" is all Harold could think to say.

Next, it was Harold's chance to practice with the power of the stardust. Mark decided to let Harold practice on the dog since the canine had no idea what was going on, and he was Harold's pet.

"Come here black," Harold summoned the dog. He then inhaled the dust from the washcloth and blew it in the dog's face which was wagging his tail happily, but sort of changed rhythms after inhaling the stardust. This was because he was feeling the slight buzz that Harold shared after having a few beers.

"Now think of black going to the door barking and trying to get out," Mark said like a paid therapist or someone who taught yoga.

Harold focused on the scenario for about ten seconds, and then the dog hesitantly trotted over to the front door and began barking and scratching the door just like Harold had imagined. The dog eventually stopped barking after Harold stopped thinking about it barking at the door. Mark couldn't help but think that the stardust should only be used on animals or maybe not at all, but he knew it definitely didn't need to be used to control the minds of human beings. Now that Attorney General Mills and the fallen angels were using it to trap people whom he didn't like, it was only necessary that the FAOA used it to even the score.

Both Harold and Martin were now ready for whatever was to happen at the club tonight. Martin was an official new member of the FAOA and Harold was a trusted affiliate. It would make Mark feel a little more comfortable about tonight and his possible temporary future in the county jail.

~

Mr. Corleone and some of his top members of the fallen angels were adjusting the lights to shine as bright as possible on Simona to give her an illuminating effect while on stage for her performance tonight. They also had Simona practicing her vocals to sound perfectly like they thought a young lady should sound to exemplify the spirit of Lucifer's fallen angels. She hated that she was involved with such a hideous organization along with such hideous characters like Mr. Corleone and AG Mills, but she knew that it would pay off big for the FAOA when they began building their case. The case was expected to advance greatly tonight if everything went as planned.

"Simona, sing each note like you're trying to fill the room with an angelic melody," Mr. Corleone shouted.

It wasn't the type of singing that Simona was used, and to make it worse, she couldn't stand to be hollered at.

She was used to singing soulful melodies with an occasional high note when it was appropriate. Simona wasn't the first artist that the leaders from the fallen angels pushed like slaves to pursue their supremacy ambitions. She was only the latest of many artists, athletes, and actors that they prepared to gain fortune, fame, and influence in society. Attorney General Mills really hoped for them to be worshipped celebrities.

They built one actress up named Lisa Jones to exceptional celebrity status a few years earlier only to destroy her career and personal life to pieces. The higher ups in the fallen angels used their connections in the news media to exploit her mishaps after hiring drug dealers to get her addicted to crystal meth and pain pills. The reason for doing this was because she let it be known that she was thinking of dedicating her life to the church and helping orphans. She went from one rehab to another, but still couldn't shake the debilitating effects of her addictions. Now, she's flat broke and lives with whichever of her old friends can deal with her drug addict lifestyle. Her old supporters in the fallen angels couldn't be happier.

"I'm trying as hard as I can Mr. Corleone," Simona stated while wiping sweat from her soft cheeks. "I really need a break. I will be tired before I perform tonight if I don't get one."

Mr. Corleone frowned at such complaints, but reluctantly agreed to allow her to retire until the show tonight. Simona walked off the stage knowing she would have to put up with Mr. Corleone's annoyances for a little while longer before she was able to get all the information she needed about his local operations. If she was lucky, she would be able to tie Attorney General Mills to the whole operation to unjustly eliminate what they called the "unwanted" of society. For now, she would anticipate a final call from Mark letting her know the mission was a go.

Chapter 21

The security guard that was guarding the door at
the club was searching Harold like he was getting ready to
enter the White House. He was the last to enter the club
after Mark and Martin who were also searched extensively
by the new security put in place after Mr. Corleone from
the fallen angels began running the joint. He didn't instruct
his security to search every guest in such a manner. It was
something about their presence that signaled the guard to
apply special precaution. They weren't dressed like thugs,
but had on common black attire, and had the look of
honest good cops which annoyed many of the leaders
from the fallen angels including Mr. Corleone.

Once inside, the three surveyed the club carefully.
Mark couldn't help but to think about how much he
enjoyed coming to the place. It didn't seem much different
than when he first met Simona there, however, he knew
the place was now a haven for the fallen angels and other
customers who had no clue what danger they was in. They
could fall victim to the predatory tactics of fallen angels
using stardust at anytime. They could come to the club
practically normal only to leave committing some
unforeseen act which would likely end them up in the
county jail.

Mark and the crew were lucky tonight. They were
able to get a table up close to the stage where Simona
would be performing. This would insure them that Mr.
Corleone would be able to see them, and would peak his

curiosity with their dark presence. It would also make it easier for him to make a fake first move on Simona whom he knew Mr. Corleone wouldn't like to engage with a character such as someone like himself.

When he talked with Simona on the phone she promised to put on quite a show with him in front of Mr. Corleone to increase his disdain of him. He knew this would set into action the expected results.

A few drinks were ordered by Mark while Harold and Martin talked a casual conversation and glancing around to see who was looking. They saw a few unpleasant characters and quite a few gorgeous women. They weren't sure what Mr. Corleone looked like, but they saw a few of the dirty cops that Harold knew from the hood standing next to security at the door.

Mark brought the drinks back to the table looking as if he was ready for whatever happened. There was music being played by the DJ that was a little different than what he had previously heard played at the club, but it was still modern pop and R&B. The new owners wanted to make sure that they didn't stray too much from the popular music listened to by the young crowd. That way they could still express their message in the music without losing the interest of the young listeners.

"If I hadn't known better, I would still say this was a nice club," Mark said. He was sipping on his drink and moving his head to the tunes.

"Maybe, but those cops in here are looking like their waiting on a riot to begin," Harold replied.

Martin was tampering with his phone and had yet to take a drink. He was focused and aware, but didn't give the indication that something was up. He just had that aura of being a dedicated military man. While Martin was tampering with his phone, Mark tapped on the knee and whispered to him and Harold.

"There's our guy," Mark said. Mr. Corleone was walking from the back room where Simona was likely at getting ready for her show. They tried not to look directly at him, but kept him in their vision from the corner of their eyes. They could tell he had noticed them, and didn't look the bit pleased. They decided to carry on like they were just the usual club goers there to enjoy themselves and see a good show. They didn't want to alarm him to much just now, but he had already walked over to where the cops were and begin talking. Mark thought that he probably mentioned to them to keep an eye on them.

Mr. Corleone was dressed in an all white linen suit with platinum jewelry on his neck and wrists. He had a thick mustache which made him resemble panama jack. He glanced at Mark and the crew for about a few more seconds then found his way back to the rooms that were reserved for the club staff.

Martin and Harold decided to mingle around the club while Mark sat back and waited for Simona to exit the backroom. While they were seeing what this new world order of a club was all about, they passed by two familiar faces. It was Mr. Cunningham from the law firm that Mark worked at while waiting to go to law school. He had Sarah with him, and was holding her tightly around the waist. They weren't all that surprised to see them, because Harold knew that Mr. Cunningham's law firm was setting up defendants for the fallen angels. However, it would still be a little embarrassing for Mark to get arrested with Sarah watching. In spite of the possibility for embarrassment, Mark would still have to carry on with the operation.

Neither Martin nor Harold spoke to Sarah. Instead, they made their way back to the table where Mark sat to notify him of the new discovery. Mark wasn't the least bit surprised either, but glanced over where the two sat. He had to get a look at what he thought would be he his future wife all over his old boss whom he once sincerely respected. He wondered how long he had been in bed with the fallen angels. He hadn't known much about the real details of his caseload at the office. Only, Sarah had access to such information.

It wasn't long after Mark contemplated on the thought of seeing his old girlfriend, when Simona was announced to begin to perform. She was wearing a glittering tight pearl white dress, and Mark thought that she looked astounding. She was already a fair height for a woman, but she was wearing pearl white high heels which made her taller and resemble a runway model. Both Martin and Harold's eyes were glued also. Mr. Corleone was already beginning to get a little agitated by the guys sitting so close to what he thought was his prize possession.

Simona wasted no time with making Mr. Corleone envy Mark and the crew. She began to sing her first song, and walked over to Mark giving him a hard stare which ended with a flattering wink. Mark look upon Simona intensely while trying not to look in the direction of the Mr. Corleone or the club staffers who were active members of his enemy, the fallen angels. He didn't want them to become suspicious of any kind of planned altercation. He wanted him to think that he was totally unaware of any kind of retaliation for mingling with Simona.

At the end of the first song Simona walked down the stairs and into the crowd. She walked among the first row of the audience casually without giving anyone too much attention, but when she approached Mark's table, she gave him direct eye contact. The eye connection was meant to make Mr. Corleone jealous, but it was hardly faked. The two had developed a bond that was destined to become realized. Before leaving the table she held the mike in one hand while she sexually rubbed Mark's chin with the other.

The sexually rubbing of Mark's chin was enough for Mr. Corleone to lose his top. He didn't even look long enough to see what would happen next. He sneakily left from the back of the stage, and eased over by the off duty cops who were still in uniform.

"What do you have on those young hoodlums sitting over there at that table?" Mr. Corleone asked the uniformed policemen. "I want them arrested for whatever you can come up with. Especially, the one that appears to be flirting with Simona," he exclaimed like a dictator of a third world country.

The cops responded hastily. "We will see what we can come up with," one of the cops stated.

Actually, they were already scoping Mark and the crew out. One of the officers recognized Mark from a picture that was shown to the other crooked cops at his station by one of the officers that assaulted Mark on the corner that day. They also knew Harold's face from hanging around their precinct area but had yet to lock him up for anything serious. Harold had been lucky not to get targeted yet. They didn't recognize Martin, because he hadn't been around the hood much since he was discharged from the army.

Two of the cops walked outside to make a few calls to see what they could arrest Mark and the crew for, while one officer stayed inside the club by the door to keep an eye on them. Simona was busy entertaining the audience, but was able to see the cops interact with Mr. Corleone. She hoped that they wouldn't discover that she was already involved with Mark. If they could make that connection, they may be able to figure out that something was up.

Outside of the club the officers discussed the situation, and decided that they would contain Harold, Mark, and Martin before the end of the club. As expected, they decided that Mark was the ringleader, and he was the one that offended Mr. Corleone by luring Simona. They were able to obtain his real legal name from the officers who beat him in front of the corner store a few months earlier.

Once the dirty cops secured Mark's full name, they contacted the drug enforcement unit of the MPD, to try to get an agent to say that Mark bought drugs from him. If the officer agreed, they could get a judge to sign a warrant before the club was over. The club would close its doors in about three hours, but Mr. Corleone could keep it open longer if necessary. He wanted to apprehend Mark tonight, and any charge would do as long as the fallen angels had the district attorney in their pocket. They would try to get him to seek no bond for Mark.

The two officers entered back into the club, and met Mr. Corleone in the back room while Simona was finishing her final song and performing what appeared to be a personal show for Mark. Mr. Corleone quietly ushered the officers in not wanting to alarm Mark and the crew or Simona about what was getting ready to happen.

"We have something on the creep that's trying to run the show tonight," one of the officers said as soon as the door was closed. "His name is Mark Johnson, and our guys have been watching him for some time now."

"Can you get him for something that's going to put him away for a while?" Corleone asked while rubbing both sides of his mustache. "I don't want to see him in this town anymore. Not free anyhow."

"We'll get him for drug charges," the other officer responded confidently. "We know he's been in areas where drugs have been sold so it won't be hard for the Judge to believe.

"Fine, move in on him when we get ready to close the club, but if he tries to leave before, apprehend him immediately," Corleone instructed. "I don't care what you do with his friends. Make it a point to let them know not to come in those doors anymore, and give this Mark character another good roughing.

~

After Simona finished her last song, she walked off the stage and had a few words with Mark. They still weren't sure if the plan had worked, so she decided to put the icing on the cake, and made sure that Mr. Corleone seen her give Mark a comforting kiss on the forehead. Mr. Corleone pretended not to be offended by the gesture, because he knew that it wouldn't be long before the police obtained Mark. He would deal with Simona after the club. Corleone's passion for Simona was based on what she could bring to the fallen angels, but it bordered a sensual addiction.

Mark decided that they would attempt to leave the club, but was anticipating a confrontation. The few cops at the door were now joined by several other cops. One was wearing a plain t-shirt with blue combat pants and black combat boots. He had his badge hanging from his neck, and appeared to have higher rank than the other cops.

Harold tried to walk through first with Mark following him and Martin tailing in the back. One of the cops immediately grabbed Harold and slammed him up against the wall. Next, an officer grabbed Mark and another struck him with the billy club. Martin was eventually grabbed, but not before he could infuse the stardust into the officers' vicinity who were bent on giving Martin another Rodney King style beating. He quickly changed the status of their thinking to put the clubs back into their holsters.

The officer in the combat boots roughly placed the handcuffs onto Mark's wrist very tightly while instructing him to not move. Mark wasn't thinking about putting up a struggle. Everything was going as planned. However, Mr.

Corleone was watching from a short distance, and was disappointed that the officers hadn't used more force while apprehending Mark.

Mark was still in doubt about what he was being charged with, but he was hoping that it wasn't murder. He knew that Officer Lake and Goldy would make sure that he made it out eventually, but he didn't like the stigma of a murder charge. Also, he began to fear that the operation would not unfold as the leadership of the Falling of Angels of America had planned, which would leave him in very unpleasant circumstances. One the other hand, he had several witnesses who were still highly ranked in the FBI who knew he had not committed any crime, because they had watched his every move.

Both Martin and Harold were asked for their identification while they hauled Mark to an ordinary police car. The cops didn't even run their name. They just jotted down their information and harassed them about leaving the premises. Mark went willingly though he momentarily looked behind him to see if he could get a glimpse of Simona. Any hopes of seeing her faded once they slammed the door on the police car. He would have to talk with Officer Lake or Goldy to find out when he could see her again.

Part III
The Slammer

Chapter 22

The holding cell of the county jail was as cold as a walk in cooler, and had the smell of old wet shoes and hard liquor. There were a variety of characters waiting to get booked or sent to their future destiny which was to the population area of the jail. It was Mark's first time at the undesirable place so he tried to keep to himself and adapt the best way he knew how, but was constantly bothered by inquisitions into his reason for being there by other inmates. Most of them had a story to tell about what ended them up in the jail. It was strange how the inmates mostly seemed to be victims themselves. Mark knew he could be considered a victim of the system also, but this time he had an entire clandestine organization that was fighting for him to overcome.

One of the inmates was an older male in his fifties and complained about how screwed the system was. He was of a medium build and had a lot of facial hair with tattoos on his arms that he probably got in his earlier years. Mark just listened, and wondered how many really deserved to be there or were there as the result of Attorney General Mills social cleansing operation. As he listened to the guy, he could tell that the older man was still physically fit. In fact, he looked as if he had lifted weights his entire life. He resembled the man from the FAOA that began talking to him in the car while he was waiting on Harold. He wondered could this be another one of his comrades after getting the impression that the man knew all about his past. He knew that there were supposed to be more undercover operatives from the FAOA sent by Officer Lake and Goldy to help him make it through this second half of the operation.

After chattering about the crookedness of the local and federal systems of justice, the guy eased back to the corner, but not before giving Mark what seemed to be a slight wink. Mark took it as confirming that he was from the FAOA, but he couldn't be too careful. There were also many members of the fallen angels spread about the jail that could easily be trying to gain his trust to get information.

About thirty minutes later, the jail dispatcher called Mark's name over the intercom. He was nervous and began to sweat from his forehead. This thing was planned, but he couldn't prepare for the fact of being charged with what he knew would be serious felonies. He pulled at the door of the jail holding cell and slowly walked up to the dispatch desk.

"Here are your forms. You're being charged with two charges of distribution of crack cocaine," the dispatcher stated as if she was a doctor giving him a diagnosis. Mark paused for a moment as if he was in shock, but was a little glad that the officers had not framed him with more serious charges.

He politely took the process sheet and walked over to the desk where they would fingerprint him and run his name through the national database. He would be lucky if Attorney General Mills had not put any warrants for his arrest in other states.

The jail officer taking his fingerprints was evidently not affiliated with the fallen angels, because she showed concern by asking him, "What are you doing in a place like this." She could tell that he wasn't really the type to be doing things that would put a person in jail. Mark placed each finger on the surface of the machine as the officer rolled each finger to get a complete print. It was official. He would have a permanent record if the FAOA didn't win the final battle. He walked back to the holding cell feeling like a criminal, but a future hero at the same time.

He joined the older guy in the holding cell in a conversation about the crooked system. He would now protest his innocence from now on until he was freed by the FAOA. They talked about the crooked cops and false arrests, but no mention of the fallen angels or the FAOA was ever discussed. Their popular discussion was frequently interrupted with inputs from other inmates about how they experienced the same mistreatment from the cops all the time. It reminded Mark of amens from a church congregation agreeing with a preacher's sermon.

After the talk begin to die down a little, Mark sat on the floor and rested his head against the wall to get some rest and think about what awaited him next. He desired to use the phone, but knew that any conversation he had would be recorded. He hadn't been given any instructions on talking with people on the outside, but to constantly proclaim his innocence. He decided that he would call his mom as soon as he received further instructions. He couldn't call any of the leaders from the FAOA yet, but he could talk to Martin and Harold in a casual conversation. He wondered if they were alright since they had not been arrested along with him. He hoped that Mr. Corleone's goons hadn't done anything sinister to them. He also hoped that Simona was okay, but he felt that Mr. Corleone cherished her too much to harm her. Mark wanted to see her as soon as possible.

~

Simona was allowed to go back and forth to her apartment as she saw fit, but her freedom was beginning to get more and more restricted since she began pretending to be a loyal fallen angel under AG Mills and Mr. Corleone. She didn't mind too much though. She was beginning to gain the trust of the families and leaders of the fallen angels. She had already reported some inside information about the fallen angels to Officer Lake. She told Lake over a secret phone conversation that the leaders of the fallen angels kept many of their important records on paper, and a report was sent to AG Mills in Washington twice a week. This was crucial, because Lake and the FAOA could make plans to confiscate those documents when they decided to make a move and close the investigation.

Mr. Corleone was fumbling through some of the paperwork when Simona walked in to butter up to him, and tried to gain some information about what the plans were with handling Mark's situation. This was the core of the operation. If he planned to try to go further with the frame up and overrule to law, then he would fall completely into the trap, and hopefully bring Attorney General Mills down with him. It would first begin with the cops who actually charged him and would appear in court with their malicious lies.

"Hello, Mr. Corleone I've been practicing a lot for when I get ready to hit the studio and record," Simona said as believable as possible.

"I think I did really well at the club the other night, other than being harassed by those guys that sat at the front of the stage," she continued. "I was happy to see those creeps go to jail. What did they do anyway?"

"They were all big time drug dealers," he replied. "The police had a ton of information and evidence on him dealing with drugs and things of that sort." Telling lies was a big talent of his. It was pretty much the golden rule with all the fallen angels although they pretended to rebuke the practice amongst the newcomers to the families. Once a member was in for a while, he would realize that the skill was praised greatly in the fallen angels as most sinful activities were. It was all just a big front.

"Oh, I bet they were drug dealers and thieves also," Simona said. She was trying to get him to say more, but he was too busy preparing paperwork for AG Mills.

After he placed some documents in a big manila envelope addressed to Washington D.C., Mr. Corleone turned around and looked at Simona. "I don't want you mingling with the kind such as those fellows at the club," he said angrily but gently. He didn't want to come off as being too cruel. He still wasn't sure if he had her trapped in his web tight enough to make controlling demands yet.

Simona nodded her head in agreement. Deep inside she couldn't wait until they had Corleone locked behind a hundred steel bars. "Oh yeah, I just didn't want to seem as if I was ignoring him. I thought you wanted me to gain as many fans as possible."

"You have the right idea, but I want you to maintain a pure image," he replied. "One representative of the high ideals that the fallen angels are all about is what I dream." He hadn't mentioned the name of the organization much since she had been playing the role of evil diva, but she welcomed it as proving their existence was also a key to completing the mission.

The fallen angels were disguised under many names amongst the various states. The heads of the families who received the money from the clandestine wing of the Justice Department were the only ones who knew the real name along with a few people under AG Mills. The President was also familiar with the name, but had no real idea of their workings. However, he continued to support it. He would be removed at the conclusion of the operation also, mainly for turning a blind eye, but the FAOA would probably not seek incarceration for him. The whole executive branch would be done away with. Many cabinet members would change to other positions in the new order of government administration.

The members in the families of the fallen angels often referred to themselves as fallen angels as if that was a good thing. They had no idea that was the name given to their organization by a Justice Department official, but they knew that their affiliation of angels across the states was some type of organized movement. They referred to each other as "brother", and could recognize one another from hand signs and their knowledge of the stardust. They also showed loyalty to the local fallen angel leader, who was Mr. Corleone in the lower Alabama. They only knew that they should look up to him as cultural leader.

The fallen angels sort of knew AG Mills was to be well respected among their kind, and many hoped that he would be president one day. He was often seen with their local leader, Mr. Corleone, and was heard to be giving large amounts of money to their cause of cleansing society of those that represent darkness.

Darkness to the fallen angels was anything not perfect according to their leader's expectations. The leaders under Attorney General Mills, who was secretly a follower of Lucifer based beliefs dating back to the beginning of America, was designing an underworld society where everyone involved thought it was their responsibility to see fault in others. Things like drinking at certain times, wearing dark clothes, or not talking a certain way were reasons to be chastised.

Simona had heard all of these things when she joined the team that was going to end the evil underground empire. The Falling Angels of America was how Simona chose to fight the society that tried to make her turn into a condemning hypocrite like the fallen angels when she was just in middle school. Now, ten years later the fallen angels were trying to mold her into some satanic idol for those very people she could not stand then. Unlike then, she now had the backing of the FAOA.

The FAOA consisted of fair minded righteous minded individuals. They had a network of units in each state where the fallen angels had sunk their claws around the justice system. Each unit secretly tried to fight the fallen angels by reducing the effect of the stardust being used to eliminate mostly the unfortunate parts of the population.

The passion for installing a righteous society where people were only subject to God and justifiable laws was why Lake and the other leaders at the FAOA chose Simona and Mark to be the new leaders of the government after they ousted Attorney General Mills. Only time would tell if they would succeed.

Chapter 23

Martin received a call at 2:30am in the morning. He was lying in bed with one of his female friends. She was a hot bombshell from the local university, and was one way he sought to relieve the stress brought on while waiting to hear from Mark in jail. The situation was similar to when he was in the military waiting to be called for overseas duty.

When he picked up the phone he hoped that it would be Mark, but the caller id read unknown caller instead of Mobile County Correctional Facility. "Hello, may I speak to Martin," a voice from the other line said. The person on the phone sounded like an officer from his old military base. It was Officer Goldy who identified himself only as Goldy, but Martin knew exactly who he was from his visit with him down in New Orleans.

"Hello, this is Martin. How are you Officer Goldy?" Mark answered.

"Fine, we have made a decision on how to move forward with the operation," Goldy responded. Goldy would now be in charge with seeing that Mark was safe while in jail, and with most communications between Mark and the outside FAOA members. The goal was for Mark to make it out of the jail without any devastating occurrences so he would be fit to lead the nation when the mission was complete.

"We need you to set up a visitation with Mark at the jail while we work to send him a solid lawyer for his defense," Goldy instructed. "You will be the person supposedly responsible for hiring the lawyer. It will appear that his good friend is trying to help him. We don't want alarm the local cops or the fallen angels of any bigger support from the outside. The case should proceed like one of the normal cases that the crooked cops and DA have been orchestrating against innocent victims all the time. If they refuse to release him once all the evidence has been presented requiring his release, we will step in and begin the takeover."

"Sounds like a plan," Martin said. "When will he have his bond hearing?"

"His bond hearing is tomorrow at 9:00am. You can attend, but you're not expected to visit him until a few days after the bond hearing. The district attorney will likely seek no bail, and the judge will probably agree at first. When we get him a lawyer we will begin to present an unbeatable case under a legit system, but the fallen angels are expected to rig the procedure."

"Oh yea, wear something dark to the bond hearing and to your visitation. It will provoke them even more. These people are real kook jobs. They get all offended by dark clothing. They really have disdain for people of color, but make exceptions as long as they abide by their rules and acknowledge that lighter is better."

Martin was of medium to darker shade of brown. He thought that it didn't seem to matter as much when he was in the military. He figured that the fallen angels' power in the military was minimal, but they probably were trying to control that also. At that thought, he knew that the operation must succeed in order to put a stop to their plan before they took it to a whole new level.

~

     The courtroom was quiet for the most part with only the Judge and attorneys speaking in turn as usual. The docket consisted of a variety of inmate characters. Some of the inmates deserved to be in there while many were there simply to push the fallen angel agenda. Mark sat along with the inmates on the side of the courtroom a little behind where the Judge's bench was located. He was wearing an all blue jail uniform with the name of the county jail stamped on the back. The blue was the color given to felony inmates, and Mark was charged with two felony crimes of unlawful distribution.

     Today would be his bond hearing. Deep inside Mark sort of wished that he could be released today after a rough night's sleep on a concrete bed, but there was no way that would happen. Once the local cops arrested you at the request of the fallen angels your chances of making it back to freedom without doing a substantial amount of time was minimum.

     He observed the Judge, and how he was handling each case. So far he had only granted a reasonable bond to a third of the inmates. The district attorney always sought a high or no bond for whatever reason. Many times the bonds weren't representative of the crime or the defendant's criminal record. Under normal circumstances Mark knew that he should be granted a reasonable bond, because it was his first offense and he lived in the state. He knew that from TV, and reading some of his law school books that he never got a chance to use.

Mark was hoping that he recognized someone from the FAOA enter the courtroom. He wasn't sure who would show, but he knew that someone was there taking everything in. They would need witnesses to all of the courtroom proceedings. The cases were called by the alphabet of the inmate's last name, which was about the only thing that was done orderly. His last name was Johnson so he would be called close to the middle of the cases which would take about an hour or so. He hoped at least Martin and Harold would come. His mom didn't come, but she knew he was in jail. He told her it was all a big misunderstanding and that she didn't have to worry. She knew nothing of the FAOA or the fallen angels.

While waiting and watching ridiculous bonds being handed down to undeserving characters, there was one defendant who caught Mark's attention. It was the older guy from the holding cell who lectured Mark about how crappy the system was. It was the one who he believed to be from the FAOA, but was unable to verify it around so many other inmates. He appeared to be disoriented unlike when he was in the holding cell when he was much more focused. The judge read him his charges. It was a charge for wondering abroad and disorderly conduct. Mark remembered that the man said he was probably guilty of walking the streets at night, and that was it. He still was unsure about whether or not this guy was from the FAOA, but the bond that the judge issued him for the two minor misdemeanors sort of increased the likelihood.

The judge issued the guy, whose real name was Simon Bradley, a bond of seven thousand dollars for the charges. Mark did the math. It would cost him approximately seven hundred dollars to bail out through a bondsman, which was ten percent of the total. Given that he was from the FAOA, Officer Goldy could have him out the same day if that was the objective. He probably wanted him to stay in as an extra eye though. He remembered Goldy and Lake telling him that he would have many members from the FAOA inside helping him out while he was locked up. Maybe they could pull a few strings and get Simon moved to his cell Mark thought. It would be nice to have someone tell him the ropes of the jail system, since Simon had been in on various times.

If Simon wasn't with the FAOA, then he was just another unfortunate person being mistreated by one of the corrupt systems Attorney General Mills had set up across the country. He had the local district attorneys seek high bonds on certain types of people as a way to keep them off the streets to cleanse society. If he could entrap them or frame them with worse crimes, he would do so, and deny them of a bond period and possibly their freedom for many years. But he was surely hoping that he was sent by Lake.

After been assigned the bond, Simon was sent out the court back to a room where the rest of the inmates waited to either enter the courtroom or waited to get on the bus headed back to the jailhouse. There would be quite a few more names called before they got to the last name Johnson, so Mark just waited and paid close attention to what was going on in the courtroom. He listened to each case closely to try to discern which ones were clearly examples of unjust treatment by the DA and cops. On certain cases the cops argued that the defendants were dangerous to society although they were only charged with minor misdemeanors. These were signals of influence from the leaders of the fallen angels.

He also watched to see if there was any usage of the stardust in the courtroom. He knew that it probably was though, because the room that the inmates sat in before they entered the courtroom was flooded with the stuff for a short period then it sort of disappeared. He wasn't sure if the inmates inhaled all the dust or the vents sucked it back in.

Martin entered the courtroom shortly before they began calling the last names beginning with the letter j and sat down in the back of the courtroom. The first person he noticed was the police officer wearing the combat gear the night of the club. The officer caught eye contact with Martin, and gave him a look like he would be targeted next if he tried to make trouble. Martin felt threatened, but he knew he was there to help his friend out with the mission.

Martin glanced over at the inmates and noticed that Mark had begun to look like he fit in. His hair had not been combed, and the jail uniform has a way of incriminating anyone who's wearing it. Mark looked back at Martin for short while, but not for long. He had learned from observing the activity in the courtroom that trying to communicate with others in the courtroom was greatly disliked even if they were there to help you. The judge, lawyers, and bailiffs were the only ones communicating in the courtroom.

A few more inmates stood before the judge to get or deny bail before Mark approached the bench. Only one out of the last five defendants received a bond that was normal for the charges and circumstances of the case. Three were denied any bond and two were given very expensive bonds.

As they called Mark's name the district attorney spoke and stated that "Mr. Johnson will be represented by attorney Cunningham until further notice." Martin and Marked both dropped their jaws immediately. He wasn't sure if he should tell the judge that he didn't want Mr. Cunningham as an attorney now or wait until he heard further from Officer Goldy or Lake. Martin was surprised, but wasn't as concerned because he knew that he would be getting the lawyer for Mark as requested by Officer Goldy. The lawyer would most definitely be someone down with the whole operation, but for now he remained quiet to see what the bond for Mark would be if they gave him one at all.

Mark stood before the judge trying to act like any defendant who felt that he was innocent of the charges. He also pretended not to be offended that the court would even consider appointing him Mr. Cunningham as representation. For goodness sakes, the guy was sleeping with his old girlfriend, but he assumed the judge knew nothing of the sort. The whole thing was to railroad him to prison for a while anyway.

Attorney Cunningham didn't give Mark any eye contact besides a few seconds before looking at the district attorney for some type of sign. Mark just decided to look towards the judge until this whole day in court was over with. He wanted to see if the judge was deeply involved with the rest of the corrupt villains.

The DA stated their case for no bond. They categorized Mark as menacing drug dealer who prayed on the weak of society to fatten his pockets and deserve bond to be flaunting around the city in his Mercedes Benz. When asked to make a statement, Attorney Cunningham didn't even offer a word. Without giving much notice as to what he intended to do about bail the judge stated loudly, "No bail for Mr. Mark Johnson." It was expected, but both Mark and Martin frowned with disappointment. Martin looked at Mark with a nod and said with his lips, "I got you homey." After that Mark was guided back to the holding

cell by a female correction officer with a long pony tail to
await the next steps in the operation.

Chapter 24

Mr. Cunningham entered the attorney visitation room at the county jail dressed in a grey suit with a black briefcase in his hand. He sat down and began retrieving several documents from the briefcase and waited for Mark to enter the room. He hoped this would be an easy process in which he would get Mark to agree to a deal and wash everything under the table. He had no idea whether or not if Mark was guilty or not. He really didn't care. He just followed the wishes of Mr. Corleone and Attorney General Mills. He had done almost a hundred cases for the fallen angels now, and had sent many undeserving individuals to prison for many years. Almost all of them got unfair sentences on his behalf, which was the purpose of his representation. He scared them with the possibility of a far worse alternative if they chose to fight it in court.

The buzzer sounded notifying Cunningham that an inmate was about to enter the room. Mark walked in with his jail uniform looking worn, but he had his hair trimmed as if he was in the free world. He had caught the jailhouse barber the night before. He really wasn't excited about seeing attorney Cunningham for two reasons. One was his dealings with the fallen angels and the other was for stealing his first love, Sarah.

"Well how are you? Have the jail officers been treating you okay?" attorney Cunningham asked as if he was sincerely concerned. "If they're not I can report it to the judge to do something about it." He tried to make it sound believable, but Mark wasn't buying any of it. He once had the utmost respect for the man when he was working for him, but that was before he knew what he was all about.

"I'm doing fine," Mark responded. He decided to hear him out. He had to at least give the system of Mobile County a chance to correct their unconstitutional acts.

"So what are my chances of beating this case," Mark asked while rubbing the edges of his thin mustache.

"Not good at all. The DA has the sworn testimony of a reputable officer stating that you sold crack cocaine to him on two occasions. In Mobile that is enough for a jury to convict. I think we should try to settle the case as soon as possible."

"Well, I didn't do it so I'm sure they don't have any pictures of me selling a damn thing unless they are fabricated somehow. Also, I'm pretty sure I have alibis for each time they accuse me of selling to the officer."

He was playing along like a real secret internal affairs agent. He was just waiting for them to dig their self deeper and deeper with claims of proof of the crimes. He knew that Officer Lake as well as Officer Paseney and Officer Goldy had documented alibis for the entire time he was home from law school.

Mark wanted to know just what kind of offer they were trying to bring to the table so he asked Mr. Cunningham, "Just how much time I would get if I pleaded guilty?"

"Well they're offering a pretty good deal," Mr. Cunningham responded. "They want a ten year sentence with the chance of parole in three and a half. You would do the remaining time on state probation."

It was just as Mark was expected. They were trying to put people away for a long time just for not fitting the profile of their agenda. If he were guilty in the first place, he was a first time offender, and ten years was way too much time for panhandling such a small amount of drugs.

"The deal sounds okay," Mark responded pretending to be cooperating so he wouldn't let Attorney Cunningham know of his real intentions. "However, I'm going to hire a lawyer to get a second opinion. Thanks for offering to represent me though," Mark added.

"This offer is only good for the time being," Attorney Cunningham stated desperately trying to close another crooked deal. "You know each crime carries a maximum penalty of ten years a piece."

"No thanks. I'm going to hire a lawyer," Mark told him for the second time.

Mr. Cunningham became very upset. He closed his briefcase quickly, and stood up. It was expected for him to get an agreement on a sentence as quickly as possible. He knew that Mr. Corleone would be upset, and if Attorney General Mills found out he would be out of some big attorney fees.

Before he left the attorney visiting room, Mr. Cunningham stopped at the door and looked back at Mark and gave him a little grin. "Oh yea, Sarah is doing real fine with me at the office."

Mark became a little furious. Was this guy insulting him about being with his ex-girlfriend, and putting the fact that he had an affair with her when he was still with her in his face? Mark couldn't wait to see the guy busted and hopefully in jail one day. He hoped he would go down with all of the rest of the vile leaders of the fallen angels.

~

Mark sat on the steel jail bed with a very thin cotton mat as cushion writing in his jail made journal. He was writing his own account of the events that were unfolding since the operation began. He was leaving out any mention of an actual operation or of the FAOA in case someone was to confiscate his belongings. He only referenced the fallen angels as the evil. He couldn't wait until Officer Goldy sent a real lawyer to help him or until the operation began to unfold.

There was a television sitting outside the cell which mostly played daytime television programs and the daily news in the morning and evening. They missed the nightly news through the weeks, because the television went off before it came on during the week. He glanced at the TV for a second, and seen a report talking about the homeless in the city. He looked around, and couldn't helped to think that at least a third of the inmates in his section of the jail were either homeless or not too far from being homeless. He thought of Simon and wondered if he would be transferred to his section. He knew he had to be affiliated.

It wasn't long after Mark began to really want to hear from someone from the FAOA, when a very large built correction officer brought an inmate in the section of cells that Mark was located in. The correction officer slammed the cotton mat, blanket, and a very thin pillow onto the floor beside the inmate. Mark glanced at the inmate for a few seconds before realizing that it was Simon Bradley, his new friend from the holding cell. The officer over the pod instructed the inmate in the cell with Mark to move to another cell, and instructed Simon to go to the cell with Mark. Mark could only guess how this happened. Maybe it was by chance, but he was sure that Officer Goldy had pulled some strings.

Simon walked in and immediately threw his belongings onto the top bunk. He didn't even attempt to argue that he desired the bottom bunk as many inmates do. Simon was humble like that, and that's what Mark admired about him. He had a good argument for being the elder cellmate to have the bottom bunk, but it didn't matter to him.

"So we meet again young man," Simon said. "It is by no means that this is by mistake," he continued while lowering his voice to almost a whisper. His beard was looking a little bit like a disguise but it was natural though.

"I kind of figured that," Mark stated. "However, you must tell me what you know before I am comfortable talking or cooperating with you," Mark added.

"I am sent by Officer Lake and Officer Goldy to help you navigate this hell hole until you're out. The first thing I am going to aware you of is that you have plenty of help from the FAOA inside the jail. Officer Goldy has managed to gain influence with both the inmates and the correction officers. The bad part is that the fallen angels have more of their people in here. Also the jail is flooded with the stardust at times. As you know they sometimes infuse the inmates with it before they go to court to secure a false confession. The inmates have no idea what they are confessing to."

Mark just listened as he thought of the various incidents he had saw and heard of involving the stardust. He thought how unfortunate it was for a person to commit an awful act that would change and possibly end any hope for a positive future.

"So, they hope to get future convictions easily handed over to the district attorney by using the fallen angel operative's use of the stardust to convince the individual to admit to undeserved guilty pleas," Mark suggested. "And, is that why there is so much of the stuff inside?"

"That's not the only reason. They won't total control over the jail to convince other inmates who have not yet became a part of the fallen angels that it is the only alternative available to them. So, when they are released, they will fall in line with the wishes of the leaders of the fallen angels." Simon began to get a little emotional. "It's a plan to destroy most freedoms of the citizens of Alabama and the United States."

"And that's why we are here to protect those freedoms that are enjoyed by most Americans," Mark stated as he was beginning to see the big picture.

Simon and Mark walked into the social area of the pod and took a seat on one of the steel benches. They were facing the cells which were lined in rows on two separate floors. Usually, inmates ate or played cards on the table, but there wasn't any card games being played at the time.

"Look over there to the right top cell, but try not to look too hard," Simon instructed Mark. There was a gang of about three guys standing at a window that was thin but long enough for each inmate to see out of. The view from their window was a public street on which cars rode by and individuals walked along.

"Those guys are using stardust to control the activity outside the jail," Simon explained to Mark while only briefly looking at the guys. "They accomplish a lot from there. They can cause wrecks or cause the individuals to go through the city creating chaos."

"How do they get the stardust into the people outside of the jail?" Mark asked.

"It's the process of osmosis. The fallen angels have the stardust trail from the inside of the jail to the surrounding areas of the jail. The same thought waves of the inmates are transferred to the unsuspecting people outside the jail."

Mark sat back and thought for a while. He knew that the stardust was a problem, but he had no idea the county jail was inflicted with its influence so much. He knew that it was dangerous in here for him. Attorney General Mills could have one of his fallen angel cronies attack him at anytime. Maybe he would hear more when Martin came to visit. He could also use some help from Harold. Harold knew a lot of tough people in the hood who were always in and out of jail. Some of his friends maybe could add a little extra protection while he was on the inside.

"Don't worry though," Simon assured him. "I spent eight years in United States Marines. I know how to survive with or without the help of the stardust."

"I'm not worried at all Simon," Mark responded trying not to sound intimidated by the circumstances. He had began to toughen from the hopeful law school candidate that he was only a year ago when he let his childhood girlfriend crush his heart after finding out that she was cheating on him. Now, he was ready to fight back and claim, Simona, one of the prizes he was promised once he helped win the battle against these corrupt forces.

Chapter 25

Martin entered the jail doors to the visitors lobby along with an attorney wearing a three piece suit. Martin was also dressed in a suit and tie. The attorney was a male Caucasian in his early fifties with a balding spot at the top of his head. He was an attorney affiliated with the Falling Angels of America and an expert in constitutional law. He spelled trouble for the corrupt officials owned by the fallen angels.

The two approached the desk and notified the desk jail officer that they were there for their 1:30 visit with Mark Johnson. The officer had them on the visitation list, but she was already notified by her superior officers to check with them before allowing them to proceed to the visitation room. She told Martin and the attorney, whose name was Arthur Grissley, to have a seat while she checked on the status of the visitation authorization.

After checking with her supervising officer the desk officer reluctantly asked for their identification to make copies. She observed the identification cards very cautiously looking for any reason not to let the men see Mark. The officer knew that the only attorney they wanted Mark to see was attorney Cunningham. Mr. Corleone had used his influence in the jail to try to prevent Mark from trying to get proper representation which was another violation of his constitutional rights.

To the officer's disappointment, both of the men's identifications checked out crystal clear. Martin had the military background in his records, but that wasn't a reason to deny him entrance although it may have aroused suspicion to have someone with former military experience visiting Mark. The fallen angels still had no idea that the FAOA was investigating them and looking towards ending their corrupt operations.

Martin and attorney Grissley proceeded to the visitation room after being patted down thoroughly several times. The door buzzed and the two men entered to a patiently waiting Mark who was a little suspicious of the new character with Martin. After having his last discussion with attorney Cunningham he was a little weary of lawyers.

However, attorney Grissley made himself known immediately and offered a professional compassion for Mark's situation. "Don't worry about these charges. It's a bunch of phony baloney," Grissley assured him. He was pretending to talk like the average paid attorney just in case they were listening to their conversation. At the same time, he was telling the truth about Mark's case. The most important details about the plans sent by Officer Goldy and Lake would be whispered at very low tones or written on a notepad.

"Now, we are prepared to take this thing to trial if that what it takes to prove your innocence," Attorney Grissley said while Martin just sat back and listened. "On your next court date they will decide whether or not it should be dismissed or bound over to the grand jury. Due to lack of evidence and the legitimate alibi of being under observation of federal officers during the time of the distributions, they're not going to have enough to wave it over."

Mark began to get a little relieved, but he knew it wouldn't be that easy. The system in Alabama under the fallen angels would hardly put themselves in jeopardy of a major lawsuit in which they had to actually compensate the people they despised.

Then, the attorney wrote briefly on the notepad in small letters but big enough for Mark to see without squinting his eyes. Mark read the words with dismay. It read that *the DA will not release you without out a fight, but we will win.*

The lawyer then continued to talk. "If they throw it out, you go home and get on with your life. If we run into a problem, then we will handle them when they occur. And that will be all for today. I will see you in court." In reality, when they won Mark was destined to be headed for a whole new life. It would be one in which he would lead a new order of American government.

The lawyer finished talking without Mark asking a single question, but harboring many inside his head. He didn't want to talk too much and put the operation in jeopardy so he just kept quiet. Martin hadn't spoken much either. He was waiting on his turn to get in a few whispers once the attorney finished talking.

The attorney stood up and pushed the button to be released from the visitation room while Martin stayed in for a few more minutes to talk to his old buddy and new comrade in the secret battle against the fallen angel society.

"How's it going Mark?" Martin inquired remembering that they could be listened to.

Mark responded "OK" aloud as if in a normal conversation. He then leaned over and began to talk in a real low tone. "How is everything with Simona?" Although Mark was in a very sticky situation with the fallen angels all over the place, he was concerned more about his future queen.

Martin whispered back, "She's doing great. She's gaining all kind of crucial information about the fallen angels in the South. She even has even given Officer Lake very detailed intelligence about the operation in Washington DC headed by Attorney General Mills. Mr. Corleone trusts her so he tells her anything that she wants to know. He won't hurt her though, but we will pull her in before he finds out she's spying on him."

"That's cool," Mark replied in an extremely low tone. "I've connected with someone that Officer Goldy has helping me learn the system inside the jail. We could use some of Harold's connections inside the jail when my cover gets blown. Talk to him and tell him to be prepared to notify his homeys in jail that their holding me illegally and we plan to put a stop to this wretched system incarcerating all our people for nothing. They don't have to know too much besides that it will pay off for them."

"Oh yeah, you can consider that already done buddy," Martin answered.

"Also, when you speak to Simona tell her I love her and can't wait until she sings me a personal melody," Mark added.

~

Mr. Corleone had decided to meet Attorney General Mills once again at the abandoned building in his home base of Mobile. The situation with Mark had begun to worry him after the legal services offered by Mr. Cunningham were turned down. AG Mills didn't think it was anything to be too worried about, but they were beginning to get suspicious that something bigger was involved with this character Mark Johnson. He began fishing around in Washington to make sure that Congress wasn't conducting any type of investigation into his dealings with the fallen angels, but wasn't able to find anything indicating such an activity.

The only members of congress who knew about the shadowbox operation were keeping the matter top secret. Officer Lake had a tight knit network of important people in congress and various government organizations that would help make the operation a success once Attorney General Mills was caught up in an undeniable wrong. AG Mills also had a network of people working with the fallen angels, which made the fight seem like a very secret civil war. Only instead of North against South, it was good against evil.

"This guy Mark Johnson may be a problem for us," Mr. Corleone stated with his hands fidgeting on the table while AG. Mills listened. They were alone for this meeting, but had several security officers stationed outside of the building for protection. They made sure they were far enough away not to be able to hear their conversation.

"Don't worry. He's just another low life loser that will get locked up and forgotten about," Mills replied.

"I'm not so sure about that. He has hired some big time attorney with ties to Washington and his friend is a reputable veteran from the U.S. Army," Mr. Corleone said. "They came to visit him the other day at the jail."

"Were you able to intercept any insightful communications concerning their plans?" Mills asked.

"No, not much. They were basically talking the normal attorney to client privileged conversation. It seemed that his friend was trying to whisper something to him in secret that we couldn't pick up on the wiretap."

Mr. Corleone leaned back in his chair and rested his fingers on his chin. He thought about the fact that Mark had suddenly left law school to begin experimenting in the streets and about his devout interests in Simona. He learned of his educational record by doing a little research, but had no idea about the meeting that took place at Virginia Central Law School to recruit agents for the Falling Angels of America.

"I think we should let him go," Corleone said. "I'm sure he will stay away from Simona if he knows what's good for him."

"There's no way we are going to start folding to these hoodlums just because they can pull enough strings to hire a big time attorney," Mills responded. He had begun to anger, and his skin had begun to get a red tint to it as if his blood pressure was going up.

"I tell you what. Leave it to me. I will look into this attorney before the court date to see just how much trouble he will be. He may be able to be paid off," Mills said while trying to cool his nerves by sipping a cool cup of water.

"Ok, in the meantime I can send him some trouble inside the jail," Mr. Corleone said. " You know, to make him want to play ball a little. And, to make him lose some of his arrogance."

When a person whom the fallen angels were trying to condemn showed any fight about themselves, the leaders of the families of the fallen angels labeled them as arrogant and trouble makers like they were just supposed to lie down only to have their possibility of a positive future ruined.

"We will talk again after the pre-trial for this Mr. Mark Johnson to see what the status of the situation is looking like," AG Mills said in conclusion of the meeting between the two backwards minded leaders. Then, the two men walked to meet their security and jumped in their cars and drove off.

Chapter 26

Simona scrambled the keys from her pocket as she closed the door to Mr. Corleone's office. She had retrieved the keys while Mr. Corleone was gone to meet some big time producers for the new record that Mr. Corleone had prepared for her to release. The producers were the same ones who worked on their last effort to gain recognition for the agenda of the fallen angels.

If she was correct, the keys went to the safe that contained a treasure of documents that showed the illegal aspects of the fallen angel's operation. Hopefully, they would connect the operation in Mobile to Attorney General Mills back in Washington D.C.

Simona tried the first key which was short and rounded on the end making it look like the perfect fit for a heavy duty safe. After inserting the key and wiggling it from side to side, the safe lock did not turn. It wasn't the key. She tried a few more keys with no success, and begun to doubt if any of the keys were for the safe. She thought for a while that it was too easy for her to get the keys that were so important. Maybe he kept the keys on him at all times.

She contemplated for a while before trying the last key left on the keychain. She gave it one slight turn to the right then to the left. It turned completely and the safe door creaked open. She quickly grabbed all of the papers stuffed inside the safe. It was also another set of keys in the safe and a few photographs. She grabbed everything and stuffed it into her shoulder bag. She wasn't worried about Mr. Corleone noticing anything gone, because she wasn't coming back. She would remain with Officer Lake and Officer Goldy until the mission was complete.

Simona closed the safe quickly, and could hear someone coming from a short distance. She briskly walked toward the door, and exited. A young man wearing all white approached her as she tried to progress up the hall.

The man was one of the fallen angels who Mr. Corleone trusted dearly.

"Hi, Simona. Are you looking for Mr. Corleone?" The man asked.

"Yes," Simona replied. She pretended not to know the whereabouts of her want to be master.

"He's gone to meet the producers for your new album. I'm surprised he didn't tell you, but that's not unlike Mr. Corleone. He always moves in secrecy."

The guy didn't suspect a thing. He grabbed the door knob to the room with the safe and pulled it to make sure it was closed tight and turned and walked in the direction he came from. Simona continued walking toward the exit of the building. She wanted to run, but knew how suspicious she would look. It would probably jeapordize the whole operation, since the documents would be very important to prove the FAOA's case and there was not telling what the other set of keys were going to open and reveal.

Simona made it to the car and turned the key on the ignition. The engine stalled on the first two attempts. She began to wish that she had her trusted bodyguard with her. He had been replaced when she started working for Mr. Corleone. She tried again, and about after ten seconds the car started. She drove away relieved and knowing that her dealings with the fallen angels were over with. No more listening to Mr. Corleone trying to persuade her that God was not real, and even worse, trying to get her to make music that would help influence the entire population of his senseless philosophy.

~

Back at the jail Mark and Simon sat in their cell playing a game of two hand spades. Mark was up in the score by two games to one. It was a good way for them to get their mind off the seriousness of the operation, but they still had to keep their eyes open at all times and watch their backs constantly.

The members of the fallen angels were numerous in their section of the jail, but not all of the inmates were from the organization. Simon had guessed that about a third of the inmates were fallen angels and the other inmates were just ordinary accused criminals, with some being victims of the unjust practices of the local corrupt system. Mark and Simon wanted to fill the jail with about a third of operatives from the Falling Angels of America and friends that Harold could get transferred to their section. That way the game would be even. They were waiting for some help to arrive at some time before Mark's next court date.

Simon counted his books against Mark's books, and counted more than Mark had gained in that game which evened the score to two games won each. They decided to leave it even, and walk out into the general area. Mark wanted to use the phone to call Harold although he didn't know if he could get his message out without alarming the jail staff, which listened to all inmate calls. He picked up the phone and dialed the number which he knew by memory from calling him frequently over the years. Harold had kept the same number since Mark could remember.

Simon sat back on the bench in the general inmate area and watched Mark's back like a comrade in the Vietnam War. Simon was beginning to age, but he could use some old military fighting moves like he was still in active duty so he wasn't worried about anything unless they were vastly outnumbered in an attack.

No one answered the phone on the first attempt. He dialed it again, and still no one picked up. Mark was starting to get a little worried. He needed Harold's help inside the jail just in case things got a little messy around the time of his next court date. Only god knew what the opposition would try.

Simon waited and observed everything inside the general area while Mark tried to reach Harold. He noticed a couple of guys frequently keeping an eye on Mark as they stood by the edge of their cells. The looks on their faces weren't the kind of looks that one had when he was waiting to use the phone next. It was more of a look like they had been planning to do something drastic once he finished using the phone. Simon was getting prepared to make the necessary moves to prevent any incident from occurring.

Mark decided to call his mom to see if Harold had called recently or had told her anything important which he should know. He dialed the number, and his mom picked up on the second ring probably worried and anticipating his call. He hadn't called her much since he had been in, because he was trying to keep her out of the whole situation.

"Hello, how are you mom?" Mark asked.

"I've been doing okay besides worrying about you night and day," she answered.

"Have you heard from Harold? I need to talk to him as soon as possible."

"No, I haven't talked to Harold since the day he came over here with you before you went to jail."

Before Mark could say anything else to his mom he felt a tap at his shoulder. It was one of the guys watching him from his cell. Simon had walked up close by, but wasn't trying to start a confrontation if it didn't have to come to it, so he waited while the man stated his business.

"Mom I will call you back later on or tomorrow," Mark told his mom not wanting her to hear it if he was going to have his first jailhouse rumble.

Mark turned around, and nodded his head upward as if to signal a response from the man to continue stating what he wanted. The guy turned around and looked at Simon, and began to smile before turning back around to face Mark.

"Don't worry homey. We're here to have your back. Harold told us that his best buddy was inside and needed a little protection."

Simon eased back with a sigh of release, but listened attentively just in case. He looked over at the other guys who were standing at the edge of their cells. They were back inside their cell talking and carrying on like nothing was going on.

"Those guys over there are with me. We're all from down the bay. We've known Harold as long as you have." The guys knew of Mark, but Mark didn't recognize any of their faces. They knew that when Harold wasn't with them or some honey, he was with Mark.

Mark and the guy, who had yet to identify himself by name, shook hands in the hood manner as if two confirm their partnership. "We're going to keep a distance from you in this cage, but if anything goes down, me and the homey's will be right there," the guy assured Mark. "By the way, you can call me dirty."

Mark went back to the cell assured that he had more help if they refused to release him on his court date when his lawyer revealed that the whole thing was a sting. Simon was right behind him picking up the cards to begin playing another game. As they sat down, Simon confirmed what he thought he heard the guy saying.

"So that's our guys huh?" Simon asked.

"Yea, we should be safe now," Mark replied.

"Oh yea, I have a little surprise coming from Officer Goldy soon. Another Iraq veteran who is skilled in martial combat. He is a big guy, and will be sharing the cell with us just in case Harold's guys can't get to us in time."

Mark was even more relieved after hearing what Simon told him. They would be ready for almost any confrontation, and they still could use their skills with the stardust to deter an attack. Simon shuffled the cards and began to deal them with a little less worry.

Chapter 27

Simona made it to the compound after a forty-five minute drive of being nervous and anxious. She had all the documents and evidence from Mr. Corleone's safe securely in the back seat of her car. There were two guards standing in the front yard pretending to be gardeners, but they wore bulletproof vests and had nine millimeter pistols stuck under their work coveralls.

Officer Lake was watching her pull up on the monitor connected to some high-tech surveillance cameras spread around the compound. He came to the front door, and gave the guards the okay to let her by. She hurriedly walked inside the building, and took a look over her shoulder as a move of extra caution and paranoia from pulling such a stunt on a notorious villain. Her hair was in a bit of a mess, because she hadn't had time to brush it after rushing from Mr. Corleone's office. Officer Lake greeted her and ran his hand through her hair to straighten it out, and then accepted the documents from her.

Officer Lake couldn't believe his eyes. There was enough evidence to prove their case for a vast conspiracy to fraudulently take the freedom from hundreds of thousands of U.S. citizens. They also had evidence of their atrocious use of the top secret government technology of stardust. They would not reveal the evidence until they refused to release Mark, which would give them first hand evidence of falsely imprisoning a government agent.

"Simona, you are truly a brave woman for apprehending the documents. I commend you," Officer Lake said in a manner more prone to a Marine Officer than an FBI agent. The Falling Angels of America were a combination of both. A partnership of the two was needed to handle the special requirements of trying to take down such a sophisticated organization as the fallen angels.

"I was nearly discovered by one of his cronies, but I don't think he suspected anything," Simona stated. "If we're lucky, Mr. Corleone won't check the safe until after Mark's court date.

"Hopefully he didn't. It would scare Mr. Corleone if he discovered the documents missing. He may begin to comply and shut down his operations. He may even be convinced to release Mark without a fight. He still will be partially in power until we can put together a solid indictment."

"I want to see Mark as soon as possible," Simona requested. She had begun to long for her new comrade and future husband who would be the leader of America soon if everything went as planned.

"We may be able to arrange something after the court date," Lake responded. "It will be a challenge though. AG Mills and Mr. Corleone will have all of their eyes in the jail watching Mark, and they will probably begin to look for you after not showing up for your rehearsals anymore. I don't know that they will connect the disappearance of you with anything other than a change of mind on your behalf."

"Yea, I should mail Mr. Corleone a letter saying that I moved to California to be with my aging grandparents. He'll probably give up looking for me."

"That's a good idea," Lake responded while he was still reviewing the evidence from the safe.

Simona got out a piece of paper from her brief and began to write the letter. She started out by greeting Mr. Corleone then she offered an apology for having to leave without first notifying him. It angered her to be so courteous to such a beast of a man. She continued to write that her grandparents were old, and had begun to have serious health problems which included symptoms of dementia. She made the letter sound very sincere in her own writing as opposed to typing it on her laptop. She ended the letter with an assurance that she would be back as soon as her cousin arrived to assume the duties of caring for them. Simona knew that would give Lake enough time to have Mark released and to complete the mission.

"Do you have a stamp Officer Lake?"Simona asked. "I'm going to mail this letter right away. It will make me feel a lot more comfortable. I don't want them to panic and begin looking for me all over the city."

Officer Lake looked in the drawer and pulled out a book of stamps. He tore one off carefully and handed it to Simona who licked the back of it and carefully put it on the corner of the envelope. She stuffed the letter back into her briefcase, and pulled out her cell phone to make sure the location was turned off. Then she pulled up her text messages to ponder on some of the cherished text conversations that she had with Mark before he became incarcerated.

"Your room will be down the hall on the left right across from mine," Lake said pointing in the direction of Simona's new residence for the time being. Officer Lake wanted to keep her close to keep a watch on her. She was a crucial part of the operation both now and after the operation was complete. She would be Mark's partner and confident as the Neutral General of America.

Simona gathered her briefcase along with the other belongings that she had brought along to the compound with her. The room was arranged neatly with a computer sitting on a desk. She also had a rather large surveillance monitor located in the corner so she could keep a personal watch on anyone trying to access the building.

She laid down on the bed to contemplate everything that had happened over the recent months. She mostly thought about her future with Mark, and how she couldn't wait to sing to him some of the songs she had been inspired to write by their relationship.

~

It was an ordinary day at the county jail when Attorney General Mills arrived in a black limo provided by the United States government. He was there supposedly to tour the jail as part of a program to ensure that places of incarceration across America were in compliance with minimum health standards. His real business there was to make sure that the jails were packed to capacity with those people who the fallen angels deemed undesirable in society. He also wanted to get some insight on the new fellow, Mark Johnson, who had become an annoyance to the fallen angel society.

He exited the limo and was immediately met by, Ike Kelly, the long time warden of the jail. Warden Ike Kelly was in his early sixties with grey hair that had begun to bald at the top. He was a very important contact to the fallen angels, and smuggled tons of the stardust into the jail each month under the orders of AG Mills.

The two men shook hands, and then they walked toward the jail's docket. Once in the docket Kelly introduced AG Mills to the members of the docket staff. Many of the employees already knew of AG Mills, and a few of them hated what they had heard about him concerning the stardust and the system he oversaw to falsely imprison unfortunate citizens.

Warden Kelly instructed one of the docket correction officers to be relieved of her duties for moment while AG Mills looked at their "state of the art booking system." The young lady smiled and departed from her computer screen politely. Mills took a seat while Warden Kelly stood and entered his login information into the computer to pull up the files of their current inmate population. The population totaled four thousand inmates in a county with a population of two hundred thousand. Eighty percent of the inmates were of minority ethnicity, but minorities only made up thirty percent of the county population. It was a fact which pointed to the idea that something was wrong with the criminal justice system in Mobile Alabama.

Mills strolled through the booking data glancing at the inmate pictures and charges for a short time. He then typed in the name Mark Johnson into the search bar. He stared at the charges and the picture for a while, and then asked the warden have he had any trouble out of this guy since he had been in.

The warden responded, "No not at all. He mostly spends time in his cell playing cards with his older cellmate. He comes out occasionally to use the phone. I don't think he knows that the stardust is even in existence in the building."

"Well, he's trying to fight his case with some kind of big time defense attorney, and his background is squeaky clean. He's even been to law school. We want him to take a ride up state for interfering with the business of the fallen angels."

"What you have in mind?" the warden asked.

"I want you to have an inmate send him a message soon as possible. You can wait to see how his day in court goes first.

Mills clicked on the close button to exit the file page, and asked the warden to give him a tour of the building including the kitchen where the food was prepared. He had to at least pretend to be performing his regular duties.

The two men continued on a tour of the jail. Mills stopped and looked through the glass doors of each section of cells. He was pleased at what he seen. His plans were really coming true. He was imprisoning all those lowlife people who couldn't represent the "light" in his eyes. The light to him was this delusional impression of one appearing to be perfect. Righteousness had nothing to do with it, and he had done a good job keeping influencing his followers to believe what he believed. He was like Adolf Hitler, but he had yet to order a mass execution to the degree of the Holocaust.

After viewing a few of the sections of the jail, he asked Warden Kelly to show him the cell where Mark

Johnson was located. The men walked through a secured door and entered another section of the jail. Mark's cell was located in the center, and it was surrounded by brick walls with a glass wall separating the inmates from the correction officers on watch.

"That's your guy talking on the phone," the warden said. Mark was chatting with Martin about his upcoming court date.

"Which one is his cell?" AG Mills asked. He thought about entering the wedge of cells to get a closer look, but decided against it.

"Cell J5. Right there in the middle," the warden replied. "He will be easy to get to." They both agreed that it wouldn't be a problem getting a rowdy inmate in there to give him a scare. If that didn't work out they could use a fallen angel to control the correction officers with stardust to make them give him a beating like the one the police had put on him while he was on the streets.

Chapter 28

The scene in the courtroom was anything but a typical day in court in the small city. The local district attorney was dressed in a custom made solid navy blue suit with an expensive tie that probably caused two hundred dollars. He had two assistants that were equally sharp sitting to the right of him. He sat at the right of the table closer to the defendants table and just a little bit from center of the Judge. He pretended to be reviewing the files and evidence for the unlawful distribution of a controlled substance case against Mark. All of it was trumped up garbage and he knew it, but he couldn't let it show to the people in the courtroom. He quickly closed the file folder with a look of confidence and looked up at the judge as if he had some solid evidence.

Mark had yet to be brought in from the courthouse holding room where the inmates sat awaiting to enter the courtroom to have their case heard. This would be a preliminary hearing, which was a hearing for the judge to decide if the prosecution had sufficient evidence to present the case to the grand jury. If the judge agreed with the prosecution, the case would be bound over to the grand jury. However, if the judge agreed with the defense, the case would be dismissed and Mark was supposed to be let free. In Mark's case, the FAOA didn't expect the jail to release him with either ruling, because of the abhorrent desires of AG Mills and Mr. Corleone.

The Judge was the honorable Mike Kraken. He was a veteran of the bench with over fifteen years as a District Court Judge. AG Mills had spoken with him on several occasions in an attempt to get him to decide in the favor of the prosecution. His last time speaking with him was the day before when he called him to decide against Mark. However, Officer Lake also had indirectly sent a message to him through a judge friendly to the FAOA. He had the judge let him know that there was an investigation into the current system in Mobile, and it was best that he ruled in accordance with the law. Judge Kraken would have to make a decision on who was most influential.

Mark's lawyer, attorney Grissley, sat patiently at the defendant's table talking with other attorneys who were representing clients at their preliminary hearing. Most of them knew their clients were doomed to have to take a plea whether they were responsible for the charges or not.

Attorney Grissley had his assistant with him, and sitting in a separate conference room on the floor of the District Court were officer's Lake, Paseney, and Goldy. They were thoroughly prepared for a showdown. Today would be when everything hit the fan. It would be quite known that the entire fallen angel created justice system in mobile was being challenged by, The Falling Angels of America, a more credible and newly authorized unit of the Government of the United States. They were authorized by a special congressional committee and recognized by a collection of judges and politicians across the country, and would eventually form a more perfect democracy under their new Neutral General.

In the front row behind the desk of the district attorney's office sat AG Mills and Mr. Corleone. Both were sharply dressed with looks of confidence that the outcome would be one that they desired. They had yet to find out that there were agents from the Falling Angels of America behind the entire event. And, he still didn't know that Officer Lake was working against him.

Mr. Corleone rubbed the edges of his mustache occasionally while looking around the courtroom every minute. He was still a little puzzled about the disappearance of Simona, but reluctantly accepted her explanation that she was gone to care for her grandmother.

On the defense side of the courtroom audience sat Martin, Harold, and Mark's mother. Mark's mother still didn't know the details of the operation, but she believed his story that he was innocent. She knew about the crooked system in Mobile designed to degrade the black youth and unfortunate people of the city. Sarah and Mr. Cunningham sat behind Mark's mother in an effort to appear to be seen as supporting him. Mr. Cunningham had no idea that Mark knew he was in with the fallen angels, and Sarah wanted Mark's mom to think she was still a decent woman.

Several minutes passed by before they released Mark into the courtroom. He was still dressed in a jail uniform since this was only a preliminary hearing. The court only allows an incarcerated defendant to dress out

251

at the actual trial hearing, which Mark would never make it to. Officer Goldy and Officer Lake had detailed the operation where he would be released before any trial ever took place once they revealed the evidence in his support.

Mark couldn't help but to think of, Job Macon, the man in Washington County that attorney Cunningham represented when he was his assistant. Job Macon was forced to plead guilty with no real evidence against him. He now knew what a "railroad" attempted conviction felt like. He felt like he was a character in the Bible being condemned for doing the work of the Lord. Although Mark expected to be treated unfairly by the justice system, he still wasn't prepared for treatment that was so contrary to what he was taught about the justice system in school. It had begun to wear on him, but he had to stay strong for the ultimate purpose.

The Judge called Mark's case after finishing a preliminary hearing for a theft case involving a stolen tablet. The case was fully dismissed, and coincidently involved a lawyer's son who had got hooked on drugs. It was one of the only dismissals for the day.

After the young man proudly walked out of the courtroom, attorney Grissley stood up while he waited for Mark to step by his side. The judge looked at Mark with his glasses resting on his nose, and read his charges.

"Your case involves a charge of unlawful distribution to an undercover agent," the Judge stated. It began similar to a bond hearing, but the proceeding would be a little more in depth. He then looked to the district attorney's desk and asked that they present their case.

The prosecutor stood and began to speak. Both attorney Grissley and Mark waited to hear what kind of made up evidence they would hear.

"Well, your honor this case is pretty much summed up by the sworn testimony of a reputable narcotics agent of the county task force," the prosecutor stated. The officer stood by biting his lips and looking back and forth from the judge to Mark, who was still standing in disbelief. He had never seen the agent in his life.

"Very well. Will the officer please state his testimony for the state of Alabama?" The Judge asked.

The officer looked over some falsified papers and looked at the judge for a hint of cooperation in the case. The judge looked at the officer with no return look indicating that he was on his side. The judge remembered the warning that he received about ruling according to the law for this case.

The officer then gave his doctored statement. "On the date of the unlawful distribution, I pulled up to the corner of Jones and State Street. The defendant pulled up in a red Mercedes and asked if I needed anything. The corner is known for drug activity. I told him that I needed a twenty dollar rock of cocaine. The defendant pulled out a plastic bag and retrieved a twenty dollar rock. I then gave him a twenty dollar bill, and pulled off."

"Is that all the evidence that the State has?" the Judge asked.

"We also had some pictures, but they were blurred by the vibration of the truck during the buy," the officer replied still hoping that the judge was bribed by Mr. Corleone. He hoped someone from the fallen angels would get contact with the Judge long enough to put him under the influence of the stardust, but it was no way to get to him. They would just have to hope that his testimony was sufficient.

The officer remained standing by the prosecutor while the judge called for the Mark and his attorney to present their defense. "Is the defense prepared to present their case for the charges against your client, Mr. Mark Johnson?" the judge inquired.

"Yes your honor, but we need about one minute while my assistant fetches some important witnesses in the case who are stationed right outside of the courtroom," Attorney Grissley stated in a very confident and professional manner.

Attorney Grissley's assistant arose from the desk and walked briskly out of the courtroom. There was a low amount of whispering from the district attorney's desk, but the prosecutor refrained from objecting to such a request on the behalf of the defense. Next door to the courtroom was a small conference room where Officers Lake, Goldy, and Paseney waited to be called.

The assistant opened the door and gladly said "There ready for you" to the officers.

The three officers walked into the courtroom dressed in their best professional attire. Each had their FBI badges gleaming from their waistline. They wouldn't reveal the entire details of their operation at this time, but they would testify that Mark was working for them while the alleged distribution had occurred, and he had no dealings with drugs.

The three officers stood by Mark and the attorney. Mark couldn't help but to smile a little and anticipate what would happen next. There were three officers from the same entity as Attorney General Mills who used to be his subordinates, but were now his superiors that were investigating his inappropriate conduct in Alabama and the rest of America.

"Your honor I would now like to allow the three witnesses for the defense to state their testimony. They are all official agents of the FBI, attorney Grissley stated."

"Did you say agents for the FBI?" the judge asked.

"Yes sir your honor."

"They may certainly proceed." The judge had begun to believe the advice he received about keeping within the law on this case was valid.

Officer Lake began to give his testimony. "Your honor we are sure that the defendant, Mark Johnson, could not have possibly committed this crime, because on the day of the distribution and several days prior he was under twenty four hour surveillance by members of an elite FBI team that included myself and these other two officers."

"Is that correct?" the judge inquired of the other officers.

"Yes sir your honor," Officer Goldy and Officer Paseney agreed while nodding their head.

"Actually he is currently working for the FBI in a top secret mission that we are not allowed to elaborate on the details at the time," Lake stated.

AG Mills and Mr. Corleone were flabbergasted. Mills immediately arose from his seat and walked toward the doors of the courtroom. He was followed by Mr. Corleone, who headed to the jailhouse to order his connections at the jail not to release him regardless of the outcome. Mr. Cunningham was surprised and upset, but Mark's old girlfriend Sarah secretly cheered the news. She still cared about him in spite of all that they had been through. As expected Mark's mom, Harold, and Martin were delighted at the testimony, but Harold and Martin knew it wasn't over yet.

The judge hit the gavel and simply said "that will be all." It was a puzzling announcement, because he failed to say dismissed or that it was bound over to the grand jury. He was stuck between the threats of AG Mills and the testimony of Officer Lake. He didn't know who was actually in power, so he kind of left the decision in the air. He wanted to keep his job no matter what happened in the future, but his announcement after the testimony of Officer Lake leaned toward sounding like a dismissal.

The district attorney and Mark's attorney both gathered their documents while the correction officer led Mark back to the courthouse holding room to be transported to the jail. Both attorneys reacted in a manner that suggested victory for their side. Officer Lake and the crew departed with much excitement. They were concerned with Mark's safety while they attempted to get the indictment against the corrupt law officials involved in the case. Officer Goldy would pull some strings to place a bodyguard from the FAOA in Mark's cell if they failed to release him.

They still had to present the evidence against AG Mills and Mr. Corleone to a special federal judge to take the fallen angels from power. One of their main priorities would be to confiscate as much of the stardust from the compounds of the fallen angels as they could. The stuff had been ruining lives in America for years now. They knew it would be a difficult task, but they were determined to win.

Chapter 29

Mark walked back to his cell where Simon was inside consulting with a monster of a guy who had placed his mat on the floor directly in front of the cell door. "This is Trevor. He's from the FAOA, and will be extra protection for you until you're released," Simon stated.

Mark introduced himself, but didn't ask too many questions. Trevor seemed like the type of guy that wasn't up for much small talk, and Mark was pretty sure that he and Simon had covered everything. He looked out into the social area for the inmates in the block, and noticed that some the inmates were looking towards his cell like he had something of value to them or like they I had something planned, but he thought that he may be a little paranoid after knowing what just took place in court. The only ones that seemed to be going about business as usual were Harold's guys down at the end of the block.

It was getting close to lockdown time, and there were several inmates in line to use the phone so Mark decided against trying to use it. Also, he didn't want any trouble. He figured it was best to stay close to his cell where he had the protection of Simon and Trevor. He climbed up on the steel bed and pulled his covers over his head after telling his cellmates that he was going to try to get some rest. He only hoped that Officer Lake and the others would have him released soon. At least he knew now that he wasn't going to be a felon for the fake charges that the officer charged him with.

Later on that night after the lights in the jail block had dimmed and the television was turned off by the correction officers, Mark awoke to the sounds of cell doors opening. In the time that he had been in the jail, the correction officers rarely opened anyone's cell unless they had emergency medical problems that required a visit to the jail nurse. He knew something was up. He jumped out of his bed, and tapped Simon on the shoulder. Simon then shook Trevor to awake the big guy in case he was needed.

There was silence for a minute, and Mark couldn't see anyone in view. Then, they heard the sound of inmates walking toward their cell. The sound was coming from the far right side of the block near the cell where Harold's people was located. Then they heard one of Harold's friend yell out. "Yo, get up Mark. You got some bad company headed your way."

All of a sudden the lock on their cell door was opened, and three guys were pulling to open their cell door. All of the guys were bigger than Simon and Mark, but none of them were the size of Trevor. They all head white bandannas tied around their faces. It was a true sign of the fallen angels.

Trevor yanked the door shut with all of his strength overpowering one of the inmates. The correction officer on duty was in on the ambush, because the locks on the door were immediately opened again. This time all three of the fallen angel guys pulled hard at the door. Trevor couldn't keep the door shut. When they pulled the door, Trevor was thrust outside of the cell where he immediately grabbed one of the guys and slammed him to the floor.

Simon had already grabbed a washcloth which contained a good amount of stardust. He inhaled a good breath of it, and grabbed one of the guys in a bear hug blowing the dust into his face while they were hugged up. The other guy had Mark in a good choke hold. He was unable to get any stardust before the guy took control of his neck. Mark was able to loosen the grip on his neck a little before the guy who Simon infused with the stardust turned and grabbed his fellow fallen angel in a police choke hold. He was under the control of Simon.

By this time, Trevor had knocked the first guy completely out, and reached in the cell to grab the other guys who were now fighting with each other. He threw them out the cell and gave them both two hard blows a piece, which knocked them down beside the other guy. Mark pulled the cell shut and tied it up with tore up t-shirts. Simon hit the intercom, and demanded that the correction officers retrieve the attackers.

A couple minutes later two correction officers came in and pulled the guys out of the block. Before they left they walked by Mark's cell and showed fake concern. "Are you guys ok," one the officers said. They were disappointed that the attack had failed. Mark wasn't expecting AG Mills to order the attack in such a vicious manner. He thought they might try to intimidate him, but that guy was trying to kill him. In the morning he would call Officer Goldy to see if they could have them released as soon as possible.

~

It took Officer Lake approximately seventeen hours from the time that the jail refused to release Mark after his case was dismissed to get a full warrant for AG Mills, Mr. Corleone, and the corrupt local officers in Alabama. The officers from the Falling Angels of America caught Attorney General Mills as he was boarding a plane in Atlanta. He had a one way ticket to Brazil where he hoped to hide from prosecution. He quickly panicked after he discovered that the confidential documents from Mr. Corleone's safe were missing. The documents implicated him and a network of fallen angel families across the country. There was detailed information revealing his influence on the justice systems across the country to jail innocent individuals.

Mr. Corleone was caught in his office in Alabama. He had too much pride to try and flee like AG Mills. He longed for his future star, Simona, whom he had begun to figure was in on the whole raid. Among the charges would be money laundering, false imprisonment, and bribery. All of the charges were felonies, and would carry a life sentence.

In addition to AG Mills and Mr. Corleone being arrested, there were many people in political power across the United States to be taken from office. President Charles Harding would be forced to resign to make room for the new position of the Neutral General of the United States. Mark would be the first person to hold that office. His appointment would be the result of being appointed in a time of a state of emergency caused by the widespread use of stardust on behalf of an evil empire run by Attorney General Mills.

The stardust compounds were raided and confiscated following the arrests. In total there were seventy two facilities in fifty states. The stardust would be destroyed at the request of the FAOA. Only a few facilities would remain open for research and the possibility that it could help save lives one day. The substance was similar to the use of nuclear weapons. It was a tool of last resort.

Chapter 30

The swearing in ceremony of Mark to the position of Neutral General of the United States reminded Mark of the day when he received his college diploma not long ago. Only on this occasion there were a slew of highly important people in attendance. It wasn't as spectacular as the swearing in of the old presidents, because the Neutral General would be a very low key leadership role. The majority of the audience consisted of people who would be crucial to the new government. High ranking military officials and members of the representatives from each state were present as well as the members of the Falling Angels of America from across the country were also in attendance. Most importantly, his family and friends were there seated in the front row.

There were a few speeches given by various participants about the importance of equality, freedom, and justice. One of the best speeches was given by Officer Lake. He spoke of his experience as the leading officer involved in the operation to end the tyranny that had begun to reign under Attorney General Mills and President Charles Harding. The audience clapped immensely when he concluded the speech.

To conclude the ceremony, the now infamous Simona sang the national anthem in a melody akin to the sound of angels singing. Harold and Martin sang along to the anthem with their hands on over their hearts. Both would be given significant roles in the government under the Neutral General.

The Office of the Neutral General would be based out of Houston, Texas, which was like a new headquarters for the Federal Government. The Falling Angels would continue to monitor the law enforcement and justice systems within the country, however, Mark would not play a role in that part anymore. He would sit in Houston in the new NG Mansion with his new wife, Simona, by his side.

Made in the USA
Columbia, SC
10 July 2022

63013088R00159